I0712469

Just One Chance

The Billionaire Barons of Texas ❧ Book Seven

CHRIS KENISTON

Indie House Publishing

Indie House Publishing

MORE BOOKS
By Chris Keniston

The Billionaire Barons of Texas
Just One Date
Just One Spark
Just One Dance
Just One Take
Just One Taste
Just One Shot
Just One Chance
Just One Mistake

Hart Land
Heather
Lily
Violet
Iris
Hyacinth
Rose
Calytrix
Zinnia
Poppy
Picture Perfect

Farraday Country
Adam
Brooks
Connor
Declan
Ethan
Finn
Grace
Hannah
Ian

Jamison
Keeping Eileen
Loving Chloe
Morgan
Neil
Owen

Honeymoon Series

Honeymoon for One
Honeymoon for Three
Honeymoon for Four
Honeymoon for Five
Honeymoon for Six

Aloha Romance Series:

Aloha Texas
Almost Paradise
Mai Tai Marriage
Dive Into You
Look of Love
Love by Design
Love Walks In
Shell Game
Flirting with Paradise

Surf's Up Flirts:

(Aloha Series Companions)

Shall We Dance
Love on Tap
Head Over Heels
Perfect Match
Just One Kiss
It Had to Be You
Cat's Meow

CHAPTER ONE

"There you go." Mitchell Baron blew out a long deep breath and for the first time in hours, a smile graced his features.

Claire stretched her back, leaning left then right. "It's never fun when the first thing you see is only one hoof."

"That's probably what Mama was thinking." Watching the healthy calf latch onto its mother was the perfect end to a long night.

"I bet she was happy to have you with her." The oldest girl in Uncle Everett's clan, Claire was only eleven months younger than her brother Devlin, and thankfully for the Paradise Ridge Ranch, one helluva veterinarian. "Glad you called me in. Hate it when I get the call after the mom has suffered for way too long. Hate it even more when we lose mom and or the calf because I didn't get a call at all."

"When she passed three hours of labor I knew something was off. Her last calf came in just over two. The way she kept looking at me, I just knew."

"That is a gift I wish more of my ranchers had. Turning the calf is not easy, but it's better than letting nature take its course and losing her. You did good calling me before the calf presented."

"I suppose it helps knowing you're family and won't tell me to go to hell for waking you up at three o'clock in the morning with a hunch."

She chuckled before her expression turned serious. "I don't even want to ask what you were doing awake all night in the barn. That's not your job." Always too smart for her own good, Claire raised a single brow at him before shaking her head and stretching her back one more time. "On the bright side, being up at this hour means that I'll be rewarded with Hazel's breakfast."

"Thank heaven for Hazel." His hand on the small of his cousin's back, Mitch led Claire toward the house. The barn had always been a place of refuge for him. As a kid when his brothers, whom he loved dearly, were in over-the-top rowdy mode, later when the stress of exams threatened to crush him, or when the senior politicians' stubbornness drove him crazy…to when he lost Abbie.

Years had gone by since his wife died, and yet, the ache was still so strong and real that some days it almost stole his breath away. But that wasn't what had kept him running home from Washington more and more. Tonight it was another text from Susan that had him seeking solace with the animals in the barn.

The moment he and his cousin crossed the threshold into the heart of the family ranch, the smell of fresh baked cinnamon rolls mixed with a hint of bacon frying, assaulted his senses. He had no idea why bacon smelled so much better when Hazel made it, but it did.

"Thought y'all would be hungry." Spatula in hand, Hazel turned to smile at the two of them. "Table's set in the dining room. Coffee is hot. Your grandfather has already eaten and is off to some committee meeting. Y'all are on your own until the rest of the family wakes."

Claire snatched a piece of bacon from a plate on the counter, and Hazel smacked her hand. "None of that till the eggs are done. Off to the dining room."

Crunching on the stolen morsel, Claire giggled like a schoolgirl.

He loved that laugh. She sounded just like his sister Eve. Her laugh would make him smile as well. It was Eve who more than anyone in the family had helped keep him somewhat together when Abbie died.

His phone beeped and he pulled it from his pocket and swiped at it, quickly putting it back. A few seconds later it beeped again. Once more, he pulled it out and swiped at it.

"Aren't you even going to see who it's from?"

"I know who it's from."

Claire's eyebrows rose up and down on her forehead a few times. "A woman?"

"Yes." He let out a slow sigh. "But not the way you're thinking."

"Oh, okay." It was clear from her tone she didn't believe him.

"Susan is only a colleague."

"Susan?" Now Claire was smiling at him.

He had no idea how she could chew and grin at the same time. "We're on the same committee. She and I were the only two on the same side."

"Were?"

"Are. We *are* on the same side, but sometimes fighting the political wheel makes swimming upstream in a river of sharks feel like an easy and safe endeavor."

"Oh, doesn't that sound like fun. I guess it helps having an ally."

Ally. That was one word for Susan. "It did."

"Did?"

Looking down at his left hand, the simple gold band that Abbie had chosen for him still adorned his ring finger. "I think Washington politics is wearing thin on me."

The humor in Claire's eyes dimmed. "Sorry. I know how much you used to love it."

"That's what I keep telling myself."

His phone beeped again and this time he looked at it.

Thought you were staying till the end of session. Are you coming back for the vote?

Quickly running his fingers over the keyboard, he typed a simple answer. *Yes.* Of course he was going back. Didn't he always? He might spend every weekend he could in Texas, but he had never missed a meeting, a debate, or a vote before, and he wasn't going to start now. No matter what, or who, chased him away.

Gwyneth Van Klein focused carefully on the small wooden

box in her hands. On her twenty-first birthday, she'd taken refuge in her father's library from the boring family gathering her mother had orchestrated. The supposed party intended to celebrate her crossing into legal adulthood. The idea was almost funny, as if her mother would ever let her be an adult. Deep down, she'd understood that even then.

Having noticed a book off kilter with the others on the shelf, something her mother would never have stood for, Gwyneth pulled the offending book out of the line. Hidden behind the row of tomes, she'd uncovered her father's little stash. Tools and materials for fine carving. They were hidden inside a box he'd no doubt etched himself. A beautiful piece of art. She would never have expected something so whimsical from the head of Klein Electronics. The discovery had the corners of her mouth tilting up in her first smile of the day. Knowing that her mother would never approve of such a mundane and common hobby actually made her a little happy. The idea that someone in the family had the nerve to stand up, even in hiding, to her mother had been her best birthday gift.

When she'd discreetly informed her father of her discovery the next day, she'd been eager for him to show her how to use the tools. For the first time in her life, she'd had something to look forward to that her mother couldn't somehow remove from her world, or worse, destroy. The unexpected reward had been finding a connection with one of her parents. As her father shared with her how to gently maneuver the sharp-tipped tool to create what she hoped would some day be beautiful works of craftsmanship, she'd actually enjoyed herself, and her father's company. But even more surprising, she truly felt that her father enjoyed passing his beloved hobby onto her. Not her brothers, her.

That time of true contentment in her life came to a crashing end when alone in his office, her father suffered a massive coronary. By the time his secretary grew curious about the lack of communication from her boss, it had been too late to save him.

That had been over a decade ago and the only contentment in her life remained the pride at finishing another work. Nora, one of the housekeeping staff, had been her comrade in arms. Nora would help her purchase the supplies without her mother's knowledge, and then arrange for the sale of the completed project in a local artist's gallery. The little money she received was just enough to keep her busy. And sane.

Setting down the sharp tool, she reached into her dressing table drawer, sneaking a snack from her sacred stash of cookies and treats. Another thing for which she counted on Nora. After all, snack foods loaded with sugars and artificial preservatives served, according to Prudence Van Klein, only one purpose: to destroy the refined appearance and slim figure of weak-willed and indulgent females. As her mother often reminded her. No one was looking at her anyhow. So what if she never quite lost her baby fat. Not that anyone would notice under the frumpy wardrobe her mother sparingly purchased for her. The only thing missing from the mid-century schoolmarm look was the laced up sensible shoes. Though in some ways, her sensible pumps weren't a far cry from the shoes she remembered her grandmother wearing.

"Miss," her name sounded, followed by a light rap on her door. It was Nora. "Your mother is expecting you downstairs. Right away. She seems rather eager."

The mere mention of being summoned by her mother for something 'eager' had her hand slipping. The tiny notch would be almost imperceptible to the average person, but not to her. As with so many other things in her life, she tossed the scarred carving into the trash. "Tell Mother I shall be down momentarily."

Standing a moment in front of the mirror, not because she had anything to admire, but because every hair and stitch needed to be perfectly in place before she descended the stairs, she reluctantly surveyed her appearance. Her sleeves were past her elbow, a true accomplishment to have convinced her mother that long sleeves were unnecessary in the miserable Texas heat. The hem of her dress—not a skirt, and not slacks, a dress—was exactly six inches below the knee and perfectly straight. Of course, she wore hose even though no one else her age, and in their right mind, would do so on sweltering days. Early in her childhood her naturally curly hair had been deemed an unruly mess by her mother. Always tamed into braids longer than appropriate for any child, now every strand of hair was neatly plastered along her scalp and twisted into a perfectly rounded bun at the back of her head. All would meet with her mother's approval. Just not a man's. At least not one in his right mind.

"There you are." As she reached the doorway, her mother looked up from her game of solitaire. The old-fashioned way, of course, with a deck of cards. "I sent Nora for you almost five minutes ago."

"Yes, Mother. I'm sorry to have kept you waiting."

"Never mind." Still looking at the cards in front of her, the older woman waved at Gwyneth to sit. "I have wonderful news."

Somehow, she felt the need to brace herself.

"The Barons are hosting the Cattleman's Christmas gala at their home this year."

Gwyneth nodded. The Barons were as far up the social register as the Van Kleins, though it was Lila Baron's Conroe pedigree that her mother admired, not so much the common bloodline the Governor had brought to the genetic pool.

"The guest list is, of course, limited to the right people."

Which meant her brothers would be on the list. Klein Electronics was only one of many corporations that continued to fill the family coffers and guarantee invitations to the most exclusive parties.

Her mother looked up from her cards. "The gala will be three weeks from Friday next."

Gwyneth refrained from groaning. Anyone would think her mother had fallen off a time travel machine. Who in today's world said Friday next?

"Your brothers have previous commitments and cannot escort me." Her mother returned to turning cards. "I've decided you and I shall accept the invitation."

Accept? Her and her mother? Gwyneth's palms began

to sweat. Dread squeezed her lungs. She didn't do well at large parties. Or small ones. People always stared at her, or more so the way her mother would make her dress. Then all the whispers would start, usually starting with *poor Gwyneth*. She hated every minute of it. She didn't want people's polite smiles with pity filled eyes. She wanted to stay in her room and work on her art until she grew too old to know that life had passed her by.

"In the meantime," her mother continued, once again looking down at her cards, "Mrs. Baron is having an afternoon tea this coming Saturday. We shall be attending."

A gala and a tea? What had come over her mother? And why was Prudence Van Klein dragging her awkward and ill-fitting daughter along with her? Something was definitely up, and heaven help her, whatever it was, Gwyneth was sure of one thing, none of it could possibly end well for her.

CHAPTER TWO

"**S**top fidgeting."

Her mother's words cut through Gwyneth's heart but did nothing to still her nerves. It had been two, or was it three years since she and her mother had gone to a social gathering. More than anything, she prayed it wouldn't be a large crowd. She hated the hum of all the voices buzzing about her ears. The polite chit-chat, the questions she never knew how to answer. *Lovely weather we're having,* of course, if she ever left the house, she'd know. *Wasn't that the best movie ever?* When was the last time she'd gone to a movie theater? The list of silent, awkward moments went on in her head.

If only one of her sisters-in-law had been available to accompany her mother, then Gwyneth wouldn't be subjected to the torture of afternoon tea at the Baron ranch. The car pulled up in front of the large ranch home that reminded her of a civil war movie; tall white columns graced the front of a sprawling three-story white brick home with meticulous landscaping.

The driver had barely come to a stop when someone opened the back door of the car. A line of valet attendants stood ready to help each guest from their car as they arrived. Another attendant opened the opposite door and extended a hand to her. Taking in a deep calming breath, she extended one leg, followed by the other, and stepped out of the car. She could do this. She had to do this. Falling over in a brutal panic attack was not an option. Neither was passing out nor throwing up, both of which were a very real possibility.

At the front door of the family home, a butler greeted

them. From his comfortable demeanor, Gwyneth guessed he was the regular butler and not temporary help for the day. Coming out of one of the side doorways, she recognized Eve Baron. A natural beauty even as a youngster, Eve always defined classic elegance. Gwyneth would have given anything to be even a little bit like Eve; not just for her beauty and style, but the lady had brains as well. CEO of her own company, Eve was as successful as any man.

"Welcome." Eve came to a stop in front of them, her eyes popping ever so slightly at the site of Gwyneth at her mother's side, before a mask of proper etiquette descended. Extending her hand to Gwyneth, she smiled. "How nice to see you again."

Gwyneth doubted that, but she was raised with the same handbook of proper behavior for a young lady. Of course no one would ever know that since her mother did all the talking.

"The feeling is mutual, dear." Prudence Van Klein put on the perfectly practiced polite smile. "It's always a delight to spend time with your grandmother." Even though Gwyneth wasn't that much older than Eve, her mother was a contemporary of Lila Baron, being only a handful of years younger. All of which contributed to her mother's archaic way of thinking.

"The seating chart is by the doorway and the parlor and music rooms are set up for the tea." Eve waved an arm down the foyer. "I have to make a quick phone call and will be right back to join you."

Doing her best to put on a pleasant smile, Gwyneth couldn't help but notice the difference between herself and Eve. The Baron granddaughter had on a simple, sleeveless sheath dress that was neither too tight nor too loose, and yet, gave the definite impression that there was a slim hourglass figure beneath the straight cut linen outfit. A simple strand of pearls matched the gold-set earrings. Gwyneth, on the other hand, wore no jewelry, and her dress, though belted at the waist, made her figure look hippy not shapely. The busy pattern of gray daisies against a light-lavender background did nothing for her complexion. Every eye in the room would be on her when they crossed the threshold and not for good reasons.

Gathering every ounce of emotional strength she had, she drew into herself, pretending she was going up to her room and preparing to work on her next project. She could do this. She had to.

Soft music, barely audible in the background hum of female chatter, drifted from the doorways into the foyer. Her mother, of course, like the monarch of a country, entered first. Her head high and a simple practiced smile on her face. Walking slowly to the assigned table, she paused to nod and greet the recognized guests. Gwyneth opted to keep her eyes on her mother and only her mother. Anywhere else and she would not make it to the table.

Several painful steps later and they finally reached the assigned table. To her relief, they were seated with Lila Baron herself. Of all the women from Houston Society, Lila Baron had always been the sweetest and friendliest. Gwyneth's mother was always the first to point out that good breeding showed. The Conroe's pedigree could be traced back hundreds of years. The objective of good manners was to make everyone feel welcome and at home. Unlike new money where showing off what one had seemed to be more important than anything else, Lila Baron immediately put Gwyneth at ease.

Already seated with her grandmother was Paige and a woman who looked almost as uncomfortable as Gwyneth felt. Feeling drawn to a potentially kindred spirit, Gwyneth slipped into the seat beside the unknown woman before her mother could suggest otherwise.

In a few minutes, she found herself sandwiched between Eve and Chase's wife CJ.

"I don't know that I'll ever get used to these teas." CJ smiled and then glanced down at the table setting. "I still think two saucers are a waste of dishes, but apparently I'm the only one who thinks so."

Gwyneth actually found herself wanting to smile. When she spotted CJ tinkering with the two spoons at her side, she leaned over. "You want the smaller one above for the tea."

Relief washed over CJ's face. "I've pretty much got the dinner setting down, but these teas always throw me for a loop."

Now Gwyneth really did smile. "I know how you feel."

As usual, the conversation around the table carried on without her. She had little to add, and when she thought to comment on a particular political situation, her mother quickly spoke over her. No surprise there.

"Lila, dear," Prudence put her hand over her friend's, "I don't suppose you can arrange for Gwyneth and me to be seated at the same table as Reginald Livingston for the gala."

Lila's gaze narrowed. "I didn't think you got along with Reginald?"

"It's his wife I found insufferable. It's no secret that the man married beneath him. But Sheila has been gone a respectable year and I'm sure he'll be in the market for a more appropriate wife."

The chatter at the table suddenly dropped in volume.

"Isn't he rather old to be looking for a wife?" Paige spoke up.

"A man is never too old," Prudence said in a tone that left no room for argument. "I would especially like to see him seated by my Gwyneth."

A few eyes popped open and quickly dropped in a too-late effort to hide their surprise. But it was Gwyneth who was struck by the shocking revelation. Did her mother finally want to marry her off to a man old enough to be her father, if not quite her grandfather?

Panic coursed through her making her head spin and her heart race, and robbing her of much needed oxygen. Shooting to her feet, she let the napkin on her lap fall to the ground and almost knocked the chair back. "Excuse me, I need to use the ladies room." Turning away, she forced herself to put one foot in front of the other and slowly exit the room like a proper lady.

The moment she hit the foyer, panic took over and she hurried to the back doorway, through the kitchen and by the time she hit the outside veranda she was almost running, not stopping till she slammed against the railways. What was her mother thinking?

Somehow Mitch had forgotten that this was the weekend his grandmother was hosting one of her charity tea events. Though he would have been fine staying in his room and catching up on work or better yet, reading a new mystery novel, he simply hadn't been in a mood to stay indoors.

Susan was coming on stronger and stronger and making it very clear she was interested in more than a working relationship. He'd tried every which way he could think of to politely imply he wasn't interested in more than collaborating on legislation. In his mind he knew his wife was gone, but in his heart he was still married. Twirling his wedding ring, he closed his eyes and brought Abbie's smiling face to mind. Getting involved with another woman just felt... wrong. Even though he'd shared those very thoughts with Susan, the woman was becoming more and more persistent. Her innuendos and double entendres were becoming less veiled and more direct. The one time she reached under the table and squeezed his knee, he almost fell out of his chair. What he desperately needed was a way to get his point across without creating a political enemy. So far, he hadn't seen a way to pull that off. In the barn with the animals, the realities of Washington DC faded away for at least a little while.

"You're doing so good, mama." He patted the rump of the mom and her calf, still thankful Claire had been here to help with the birth.

"Hiding out?" Mack, their longtime foreman, came out of one of the stalls. "Lord knows I appreciate a good woman, but twenty or thirty all yacking at once is just a bit much."

Mitch chuckled. The guy had a point. "Just checking on mama and her calf."

"She's been doing real good." Mack hung a harness in

the tack room and closed the door behind him. "If you don't need me for anything, I'll be heading home."

"No, thanks. I should be getting back to the house too." He scratched the mama cow behind the ear for a second and turned to follow Mack out of the barn. If he slipped in the kitchen door and up the back stairs, none of the guests would even know he was home.

Lost in his thoughts of Susan and how to untangle the mess that had been building the last year or so, an odd sound caught his attention. Slowing his pace, he strained to hear, unsure from what direction the noise was coming. A few more paces and the sound became clearer. Could it be crying? And coming from the veranda? Fearful it was one of his sisters, or sisters-in-law, he picked up the pace, the sound growing stronger. Most definitely a woman crying. As he reached the foot of the stone steps, he could see a figure leaning over the railing, swiping at her face. Definitely not one of his sisters or in-laws.

Unsure if his presence would be appreciated, but unable to walk away from a woman in distress, he slowly approached her. "Is everything all right?"

Caught off guard, the woman spun around, her eyes round as saucers and her hand swiping madly at her eyes. "I thought I was alone."

Gwyneth. He dared to step in closer. "I was in the barn."

Her head turned left then right, one hand swiping at her cheeks, the other fussing in a pocket. Then she quickly switched hands and searched the other pocket before straightening her back. "I don't suppose you have a tissue?"

That had to be the longest sentence he'd ever heard her utter. Even a million years ago at her party, all he'd gotten was that soulful *thank you* at the end of the night. Without hesitation he pulled out the handkerchief he'd kept in his pocket for just such an occasion. "Here you go."

"No." She shook her head. "I meant a disposable."

He gave her an easy smile, hoping it would help somehow. "My whole life the Governor and Grams have made us carry a spare handkerchief just in case. Until this moment, I've never actually needed to share it with a distressed damsel. Please don't deny me the opportunity to make my grandparents proud."

The corners of her mouth started to tip up before tears welled in her eyes and her head bobbed. "Thank you." She wiped away the tears, dabbed at her nose and folding it gently in her hands, slid it into her pocket. "I'll have it washed and returned to you."

"No need." He shook his head. "I have a drawer full of them."

Lips pressed tightly together, she seemed to be desperately trying to pull herself together.

"I don't mean to intrude, but what has you so upset?" The last thing he wanted to do was upset Gwyneth even more, but the simple question worked like turning on a faucet. In seconds tears were pouring down in earnest.

She quickly spun around, pulled the hanky out and swiped at her eyes again. "It's nothing."

A smart man would have accepted her response and walked away, but Abbie would have boxed his ears for not at least trying to help. He dared to get even closer, but resisted the urge to pull her into a gentle hug and comfort her the way he would have one of his sisters after falling off a bike and skinning a knee. "Doesn't sound like nothing to me."

Sucking in a ragged breath, she twisted ever so slightly to face him. "It's Mother."

He bobbed his head. No surprise there. He'd always suspected she had a difficult life under Prudence Van Klein's thumb; now he was sure. "I see. What did Prudence do?"

Tears welled in her eyes again and she blinked them back frantically. "She wants me seated next to Reginald Livingston at the gala."

"Why?" Even to him that seemed an odd request.

"She thinks he's in the market for a new wife."

He wasn't sure if his jaw hit the floor but he was positive his eyebrows were brushing his hair line. "You?"

Gwyneth sucked in another breath and nodded.

"That's insane." Suddenly it occurred to him that she

might think he was referring to the idea of her as a wife and not Reginald as a husband. "That old goat could be our father."

"I know."

At least she had the good sense to realize what a crazy idea a match like that was, but he feared she'd never have the nerve to stand up to her mother. If she did, she would have broken free ages ago.

"There you are." Prudence Van Klein stood ramrod straight by the doorway to the family dining room. "I've been looking for you."

"I… uh… needed a little fresh air."

"Well. This is no time for lollygagging. Lila has been quite gracious inviting us and it's quite rude to sneak out like this."

"Yes, Mother." Gwyneth shifted as if ready to follow her mother back inside, but didn't seem to be able to move one foot in front of the other.

"I do have good news. Lila has agreed to seat you with Reginald at the gala."

"Oh." A hint of panic flickered in tearful eyes and Mitch could hear Abbie's voice in the back of his head shouting, *Do something!*

"I'm afraid that's impossible." Mitch inched closer to Gwyneth.

He wouldn't have thought it possible for Prudence to stand any straighter, but somehow his contradiction stretched her height another inch. "And why is that, young man?"

"Gwyneth has agreed to be *my* date for the gala."

CHAPTER THREE

Gwyneth had never seen her mother sputter before. Clearly startled, the woman's mouth kept opening, wanting to respond, but nothing came out other than an occasional squeak. Even Gwyneth wasn't sure she'd heard correctly.

"I'm sure my grandmother will be happy to still seat you with Reginald," Mitch spoke as if her mother weren't on the verge of apoplexy. "But I'll need Gwyneth at my table. I hope you understand." As if to show he was immovable in his statement, he took yet another step closer to Gwyneth, sidling up close enough for her to feel his warmth and get a good whiff of his cologne.

"I…I." Prudence looked from Mitch to her daughter and back. "Had better get back inside and inform Lila of the change in plans." For a woman of her years, she spun around easily and pausing a moment, tossed over her shoulder. "Don't dawdle, Gwyneth."

Not till Prudence was inside the house and the doors latched completely closed, guaranteeing she was no longer within listening distance, did Gwyneth dare face Mitch. "Why did you do that?"

"I apologize for being presumptuous, but surely accompanying me can't be more distasteful than sitting with Reginald Livingston?"

Did he actually mean for her to be his date? Or was she so obviously pathetic that he felt obliged to sacrifice himself in a pity date?

"Uh, oh. Did I misunderstand? Did you want to be seated with Livingston?"

Her head shifted from side to side so quickly, it was a

wonder her brains weren't falling out of her ears.

"Then you'll accept my brazen invitation?"

This time her head moved up and down, but her voice seemed to have shriveled up. Pity, concern, chivalry, whatever the reason for his gesture, she was too relieved to turn him down.

"Good." He smiled at her. "May I have your number? To give you a call with more information."

"I… don't have my own phone." How lame was that. Everyone and their godmother had their own cell phone, but her mother saw no need for it. Frankly, neither did she. After all, who would she call?

His head tipped slightly to one side, no doubt pondering just how archaic her world was.

"You can reach me on the family landline." Her hands patted her pockets. "I don't have a pen or paper."

"Neither do I." He pulled out his phone, tapped in the number she gave him, then took a step back. "I'll call you when I have more details, but for now, I'd better let you get back inside before your mother bursts a blood vessel."

It shouldn't have, but his uncanny and accurate observation made her laugh. "Yes. Thank you."

Content with the sudden shift of events, and feeling free of her mother's scheming, she'd made it all of two feet inside the Baron home when reality struck her in the solar plexus. What had she agreed to? Mitchell Baron was a United States Senator. A Baron, the closest thing to American royalty. Photographers followed him everywhere, and this gala would be no exception. He would be photographed all night along with her. Frumpy her. No way would her mother allow her to buy an appropriate dress. Worse than that, no way would a simple dress be enough to make her look like she belonged at the senator's side. Gwyneth remembered Abbie Baron too well. The woman was slender, smart, and stunning.

Quickly her mind ran through years of newspaper articles on the golden boy senator. Not since his wife had she seen a woman at his side. Why now? Why her? Her steps slowed. Could this be a joke? A horrible practical joke? No. She shook her head. Mitch was a kind man. A good man. She'd known that ever since her coming-out party. A few years older than her, he'd been roped into escorting her by his grandmother. She'd been embarrassed, scared, and uncomfortable. He'd been kind, considerate, and at her side all night. He wouldn't use her as the brunt of a bad joke. He had to be serious. After all, he'd asked for her phone number.

The hum of women's voices flowed from the tea room and once again she was struck with the cold reality of her situation. Frumpy, overweight, boring, ugly, and unattractive, she was about to make the biggest fool of herself yet. Worse, what would people say about Mitch for being with her? Suddenly, she felt as sorry for Mitch as he must have felt to find her crying on the veranda. What had she gotten into?

"You look a bit green around the gills." The tea over and all the chattering women gone, Mitch's sister Eve came up behind him.

Since inviting Gwyneth to the gala, he'd remained outside, leaning over the railing, staring out at the rolling hills of Paradise Ridge, asking himself when had life become so darn complicated?

Eve sidled up beside him and leaned her arms over the rail, mimicking her brother's pose. "You have accomplished something few people can manage."

Tilting his head, he slanted a questioning gaze in his sister's direction.

"Prudence Van Klein is at a loss for words."

"Well, there is that." He blew out a sigh and fully faced his sister. "Is she giving Gwyneth a hard time?"

"She's not giving anyone a hard time. She merely sat down, looked at Grams and told her that Gwyneth would be seated with you."

"What did Grams say?"

"Nothing, she just smiled."

"Smiled? What does that mean?"

Eve shrugged. "I'm not a mind reader."

It had been an awful lot of years since he was a young man escorting Gwyneth to a party or since the Governor had set his brother up with the sheltered young woman at one of Mitch's fundraisers. "Surely, Grams isn't thinking this is a real match?"

"Don't know that either. But I do believe the Governor will have an opinion on this that he won't try to hide."

Unfortunately, Mitch agreed with her. He hadn't really thought ahead about any of this. The two stood looking out in silence for several long moments.

"Care to share what the heck actually happened out here?" Eve continued to stare ahead.

"I honestly don't know. I found her standing here crying. If I'm reading the room correctly, after years of stifling any possible chance of Gwyneth finding a good husband, or a career, or a life of her own for that matter, Prudence wants to hook the poor woman up with one foot in the grave Reginald Livingston."

Eve sighed and bobbed her head. "Seemed that way to me too."

Holding on to the railing, he pushed to a standing position. "She was so sad, it brought back memories of the quiet young woman who looked up at me with soft grateful eyes and said *thank you* after her mother had thrown a traditional debutante ball reminiscent of a long-ago era, introducing their only daughter to society. Then I remembered the way you and Chase talked about her on the yacht during Andrew's wedding days. I'm sure there are plenty of others who look down on her."

Eve nodded at him. "She is a bit of a misfit."

That was putting it nicely. "I had to do something. I opened my mouth and telling Prudence that Gwyneth had agreed to be my date for the gala was what came out."

"I see."

"Do you think I made a mistake?" If he thought he was confused about how to deal with Susan, this was a whole new ballgame. "Women can be so complicated, and this situation is going to be awkward at best with a strong chance of fiasco. I don't want to make things worse. She doesn't deserve that."

"I honestly don't know." Eve pushed away from the railing. "I don't know her well enough to presume anything, but I can't even imagine what it must be like to live under the watchful eye of Prudence Van Klein, and the thought of being pawned off on a man nearly twice my age is even more frightening. I don't think she has any friends that I know of, but if anyone can use a knight in shining armor it's that woman."

"I'm not anyone's knight in shining armor."

"Maybe, maybe not. Perhaps a good friend wouldn't be a bad goal?"

Could he do friends with Gwyneth? He thought he could do friends with Susan and look where that got him.

Eve shifted her attention to her brother. "Right about now, if I were her, I would be doing a dodged-that-bullet jig of happiness."

"It's just one gala."

"Until the next time you get wind of one of Prudence's heavy-handed plans for her daughter." Eve took a step in retreat. "Whatever you decide, if I can be of any help, just whistle."

"Thanks." He didn't even know where to begin. Talking to the woman when she wasn't crying her eyes out might be a start. It would probably take her and her mother a good thirty minutes to arrive home. Would calling her today send the wrong message?

CHAPTER FOUR

To Gwyneth's surprise, her mother did not say a single word the entire drive home, with the exception of telling the chauffeur that she would not be needing him or the car the rest of the day.

That suited Gwyneth just fine. At this moment she was so confused, she wouldn't have known what to say if her mother had started asking questions. Thoughts, emotions, and fears were wrestling about inside her like a harem of women in a mud bath. Tired, dirty, battered and bruised, no clear winner was in sight. If she thanked Mitch for his kind offer but declined the invitation, then her mother would get right back on the idea of sitting her with Reginald Livingston. On further thought, that might not be so awful. Before her mother had developed a preference for her son and daughter-in-law's company at social events, Gwyneth had accompanied her mother, and none of the eligible men she'd crossed paths with back then had shown any interest in her, why would Mr. Livingston be any different?

But what if he did? Then what would she do? Maybe Reginald was a nice man. Old, shriveled, but nice. Companionship could be good. Unless the old goat was neither nice, nor interesting, nor companion material, and just like that the mud wrestling match in her mind continued with no clear winner.

Inside the house, her mother removed her wrap and handed it to their butler. "Oliver, if you would see to it that Miss Gwyneth and I are served coffee and a cheese and charcuterie platter in my room. I'm quite fatigued." Chin high, she turned to her daughter. "I shall expect you in my room once you've freshened up."

"Yes, ma'am." So much for escaping the inquisition. She should have known her mother would not air their laundry in front of anyone, not even the driver.

From the kitchen, the ringing of the phone could be heard. She'd barely made it to the foot of the stairs, only a few steps behind her mother, when Oliver reappeared.

"A call for Miss Gwyneth. Senator Baron." If the man was at all surprised at Gwyneth getting a phone call, his stoic expression hid it well. "Shall I tell him Miss is not receiving calls?"

"Thank you, Oliver. That would be—"

"I'll take it in the library, Oliver. Thank you."

If it were physically possible for her mother to shoot daggers at her daughter, she would be. Her gaze was angry and annoyed for a heated moment before a curtain of civility descended and she nodded to Oliver. All of Gwyneth's life she'd not been allowed to make a single decision on her own. When she'd shown interest in going to college, her mother had quickly deemed it unnecessary. When she'd suggested working for the family business, her mother had been nearly apoplectic. Arguing that it was good enough for her brothers, why not for her, had been a waste of Gwyneth's energy. She'd had no friends, her mother had not cared for the free hand her generation had been shown, hence nothing to do and nowhere to go. Though escaping on her own once she reached the age of maturity had fleetingly crossed her mind, she hadn't found the courage to risk homelessness without a dime to her name or a marketable skill set.

Standing by her father's old desk, reaching for the receiver of the ornate replica phone, she tried so very hard not to let her hand shake. Especially when she heard the click of the door latch behind her. It should have been no surprise that her mother would follow her. Privacy was not a luxury she was entitled to.

Phone to her ear, she willed herself to calm down. "Hello."

"Gwyneth, hello again."

Had his voice always been so soothing?

"I hope I'm not disturbing you."

She shook her head before realizing words were necessary. "No."

"Good." He paused a moment, she wasn't sure why. "I thought it might be a good idea to chat about today and the gala."

"Yes." She supposed that was as good an idea as any.

Another long moment of silence hung in the air. "Are you alone?"

"No."

"Your mother?"

"Yes."

"I see." This time she heard him sigh. "Listen, I know it's short notice, but are you free for a bite to eat? I could pick you up for dinner in about..." He paused again, perhaps looking at a watch, or reminding himself that he was crazy for asking her out. "An hour and a half. Would that work?"

She stared silently at her mother. The woman showed no emotion of any kind. If Gwyneth ever needed a backbone, it was now. "Yes. That will be fine."

"Good. Good," he repeated. "I'll see you then."

"Yes."

"Goodbye for now."

"Yes. Goodbye." She slowly placed the receiver in the handset, afraid to lift her gaze.

"Since when do you talk to the Senator?" Her mother had not moved from the doorway.

The woman could spot a lie a mile away. Gwyneth had to be careful in her choice of words. "I've known the Senator, Mitchell, for years. You know that, Mother."

"Yes, well." Her mother huffed and barely shook her head. "That still doesn't explain today."

No, she supposed it didn't. Evasion might be better than a defensive position. "I need to freshen up. He's picking me up for dinner."

Her mother's eyes popped open wide and her jaw dipped slightly open before snapping shut.

With all the strength she could muster, she put one foot

in front of the other and marched toward her mother and the door. "If you'll excuse me."

Blinking, her mother took a step sideways and allowed Gwyneth to exit the room. Maybe she should have grown a backbone sooner.

Mitch turned the corner of the street the Van Klein estate was on and realized he'd been shaking his head for the last few miles. When he had Gwyneth on the phone, he couldn't decide if her one word responses were an improvement over an evening of silence when she was sixteen or forced to accompany Craig to one of Mitch's fundraisers, or if Prudence had the woman scared silent.

The only way he would find out was getting her away from the house and trying to uncover what she was thinking. Much like the declaration about the gala, the invitation to dinner had simply slipped out of his mouth before he'd had a chance to consider the implications or consequences. He hadn't asked a woman out—under any circumstances—since Abbie. The mere thought of taking that step paralyzed him, and yet, even though the invitation had been impulsive at best, and perhaps even a bit confusing, for whatever reason, he knew saving Gwyneth from her mother's pitiful matchmaking choice was the right thing for him to do. He also knew that Prudence was too well bred to create a scene in public, or in the presence of a United States senator. At least he hoped that would be the case.

Announcing himself at the front gate intercom, he tried not to squirm waiting for someone to open the iron gates. For a brief moment, it crossed his mind that Prudence would simply put her foot down and not allow him anywhere near the house. Relief washed over him when the ornate ironwork finally began to slowly swing forward.

Another moment and he was bounding up the steps to an already open front door.

"Miss Gwyneth is expecting you." The family butler stood to one side and waived him forward.

Following the man, Mitch discreetly surveyed the surroundings. The house looked more like a mausoleum than a home. He hadn't seen anything so ornate in anything other than a black and white movie. Even the White House, in all its splendor, wasn't such a throw back to another era. Ahead of him, the butler opened another set of doors and seated in a room straight out of a Louis XV recreation, Prudence Van Klein appeared to be holding court. Gwyneth, on the other hand, sat with her hands folded, and her gaze to the floor.

Anger at how badly she'd been beaten down threatened to overcome his good manners and let him give Prudence a very large piece of his mind. Instead he settled for forced politeness. "Good evening, Gwyneth, Mrs. Van Klein."

"A pleasure to have you in our home," Prudence replied. Her daughter's gaze still cast downward.

"Greater still is the pleasure of your daughter's company." He turned to Gwyneth. "If you're ready, I have reservations and don't want to be late." Before either woman could respond, he turned back to Prudence. "I hope you'll forgive my hurrying Gwyneth away, but you know how difficult reservations can be to get, even for a senator."

Much like earlier in the day on the veranda, Prudence seemed ruffled by another person taking control of the room and the conversation. "Yes, of course."

It struck him that she had probably been used to holding tight reins on everything since her husband died all those years ago.

On her feet, Gwyneth allowed her gaze to meet his. He couldn't be sure but he thought he saw relief, and like that night all those years ago, gratitude. Without hesitation, he extended his elbow to her, pleased when she easily accepted.

Taking his time, they crossed the room, entered the foyer, and left the house. Almost the entire time, he could feel the gazes of both Prudence, the butler, and probably some other hidden staff, burning against his back. Not till he had Gwyneth seated and himself settled behind the wheel and the car out of the estate grounds did he dare speak. "Thank you for accepting my invitation."

She nodded, but not a word came out of her mouth.

If the rest of the evening was going to move along, as in past experiences with him doing all the talking, this was going to be a long and fruitless meal.

"May I ask where we're going?"

The sound of her voice almost startled him off the road. "I may have fibbed to your mother."

For a second he thought he saw a hint of a smile teasing at one corner of her mouth.

"I have not made reservations. I thought you might have a favorite place you'd like to go to."

That glimmer of a smile instantly disappeared, followed by a soft sigh and shake of her head.

"Do you have a favorite kind of food?"

Her one hand squeezing the fingers of the other on her lap, she shook her head again.

This was going to be difficult. He was torn by how she looked almost as afraid of dinner with him as she had been sitting in a room with her mother. Did she prefer quiet and sheltered, or crowded where she could blend in with the crowd? Not that she would blend in anywhere. Her dress was almost to her ankles, and the collar covered an inch or two of her neck. She truly looked like someone's grandmother about to attend a dreaded funeral.

"I do like pasta." Her voice came out so soft and low as she spoke facing the dashboard, he almost didn't hear her.

"Perfect. I know an excellent little Italian restaurant and it's not far from here." And if God were on his side, it wouldn't be crowded. Then he could get his usual table in the back, away from gawking eyes, and conducive to private conversation. Now all he had to do is figure out what the heck he was going to say.

CHAPTER FIVE

"**S**enator." The owner of the Amore Café came hurrying out from behind the kitchen counter to greet him. "So happy to have you join us. Your usual table?"

"If it's available, please."

"Of course." The man grabbed two menus and rather than walk them through the middle of the restaurant, took them around the side and across the back to the far booth. "Your server will be here shortly."

"Thank you, Vinny."

The way Gwyneth held the menu in front of her, studying the contents as though the waiter might be giving a pop quiz, he had no idea if she was truly that engrossed or trying desperately to avoid looking at him and igniting a conversation. Not till the waiter appeared at her side did she finally look up. Another few minutes and their orders were placed, the waiter retreated to the kitchen and the two of them sat staring in silence.

"You're going to love their lasagna. Vinny uses his grandmother's recipes."

"It's a favorite."

He waited a beat to see if she was going to say something else and quickly realized he was going to have to pull conversation from her. "I always have a hard time choosing between the lobster ravioli or the chicken parmesan. My wife used to tell me that I needed to branch out more, try new things."

"Abbie was very kind."

"She was."

"You miss her still, don't you?" For the first time since

he saw her seated in her front parlor, Gwyneth's shoulders relaxed.

"Every day." Now he was the one who didn't have more words.

"I remember her from school."

He paused. His mind going back in time to the all-girls high school Abbie attended. Or did Gwyneth mean college?

"She was a year ahead of me in high school. Every so often we'd pass in the halls. She was so beautiful."

That she was.

"She always smiled at me."

Abbie had a beautiful smile.

"Most people pretended not to even notice me."

And just like that, his mind abandoned a walk down memory lane and circled around to the issue at hand. "Are you okay accompanying me to the gala?"

Gwyneth's eyes drew closed for longer than a blink; finally she sucked in a deep breath, opened her eyes and nodded.

"Am I that off-putting?"

"No!" She shook her head. "I didn't mean… It's just… I mean…"

"I don't bite. Just spit it out."

Her hands clasped in front of her, she glanced down at her fingers then back up at him. "I'm an embarrassment."

"Who told you that?"

The scared child expression fell away, replaced by a look that could only say how stupid are you. "No one has to tell me anything. One look in the mirror is all I need to know that I will not fit into your world."

Wow. He finally got a multi-sentence response from her and it was loaded with all sorts of landmines. "That's simply not true."

One eyebrow shot up. So the country mouse had a bit of gumption. "Have you looked at me?"

"Is that a trick question?"

She rolled her eyes and leaned back, arms spread wide. "Can you imagine any of your sisters in a dress like this?"

Now that he'd opened Pandora's box, apparently

Gwyneth had quite a bit to say. "It might not be their style."

"Style? There is no style. Just look at me." Blowing out a deep sigh, she sank back in the chair. "Maybe I should just let Mother have her way and sit with Mr. Livingston."

It was beginning to dawn on him that Gwyneth's issues would not be solved by a single outing with him to one of the social events of the year. He also had to admit that like it or not, she had a point. If she attended the gala in anything akin to what she was wearing now, she would indeed attract all the wrong kind of attention. For himself he didn't care, but he didn't like the idea of tongues wagging on his watch. "If you don't like your dress, why not wear something else?"

"If Mother is going to pay for my clothes, than Mother gets to pick what I wear. Mother doesn't approve of dresses above the knee, Mother does approve of sensible shoes, Mother doesn't see fit for me to be seen with people beneath our social standing, which, of course, means I don't get to see anyone. If she didn't respect and admire your grandmother so much, she probably wouldn't have let me out the door even with you. So no, I don't get to pick something else to wear."

"But you'd choose something different if it were up to you?"

"If it were up to me, I'd look like your sister Eve, but it's not up to me." A self-deprecated laugh bubbled unexpectedly. "Not that there's a dress on this planet that would make me look like one of your sisters."

Not sure what to say, he was thankful for the appearance of a waitress with two salad plates in hand. As the young woman set the dishes in front of them, he took a moment to study Gwyneth. At first glance she was indeed plain and rather drab, but the longer he looked at her, the more he noticed. Alabaster skin accented a classic profile with high cheek bones. Nervous fingers that she tended to clasp almost in prayer, were long and slender, worthy of a concert pianist. Lips that rarely smiled were a lush pale pink that many a woman paid a pretty penny to imitate.

Another of the waitstaff appeared with a pitcher of

water and began refilling their glasses once the other waitress withdrew from the table. As Gwyneth reached for her water, long slender fingers encircled the tall glass. Even with her nails bare and unpolished, she had lovely hands. Stalling over a slow drink of water, he had to admit, Gwyneth had the foundations of a beautiful woman. Her mother had merely buried it under a dowdy persona.

If only Abbie were here, she'd be able to tell him what to do. "Do you like shopping?"

"Excuse me?" Gwyneth hadn't meant to lay her cards on the line. As a matter of fact, she'd been a bit shocked to hear her own voice actually saying out loud the frustration she'd felt for most of her life, but she couldn't stop. Every word out of Mitch's mouth only flamed the fires of her irritation with what her life had become. She had no idea why Mitch was different from any other person she'd ever had to spend silent time with, but talking to him was as comfortable as talking to herself. Perhaps it was because in an odd way, even if only for one night, Mitch had been the only person she might consider a friend. And for that very reason, it wasn't fair for him to be saddled with her.

He glanced at his watch. "It's still early. What do you say after dinner we hit the mall and do a little window shopping?"

Had the waiter spiked Mitch's water? What man wanted to window shop on a Saturday night? With her, no less. "Why?"

"Why not?" The man had the nerve to smile at her. Really smile. Big and wide, and oh how those baby blues twinkled when he grinned. "It could be fun."

"Have you ever been shopping in a mall on a Saturday night?"

"Not since high school, but how awful can it be?"

If she'd ever been out shopping in a public mall, she might have an answer for him, but her mother stopped taking Gwyneth shopping in junior high. "I guess we're going to find out."

Mitch leaned back with a satisfied smile and not for the first time she wondered if he'd lost his mind. No one wanted to spend time with her.

At that moment the waiter brought their entrees.

"Thank you," Mitch said to the young man, then leveled his gaze with hers. "Bon appetite."

"Toi aussi."

His brow shot up. "You speak French?"

She swallowed hard, not having meant to respond that way. "A little."

"Where did you learn?"

"One of those self-taught programs."

His fork dangled in mid-air. "Really?"

"Really. It went well with Spanish so I thought I'd try French."

"French and Spanish?" He dabbed at the corner of his mouth with his napkin. "That's impressive."

"Thank you." She couldn't help but smile. She'd used some of her craft money to buy a tablet and the language programs. Once she'd more or less mastered French and Spanish she considered trying German, but in the end decided what good did it do her to speak foreign languages if there wasn't a snowball's chance in hell she'd ever get to travel and use them.

To her surprise, talking through dinner came more easily than she'd expected. Mitch was easy to talk to, didn't look down on her, didn't criticize, didn't tease or make fun of her, and best of all, seemed to actually be interested in what little she had to say. When the waiter took the near empty dishes away, they declined dessert and as soon as Mitch paid the bill, they were up and out the door and on their way to the nearest shopping mall.

It should have been no surprise to her when he pulled up outside a major exclusive department store and circled the car to open her door. "Ready?"

No was probably not the response he wanted. Taking hold of his hand, she exited the car and wondered what the heck did he have in mind? She had no purse, and even if she had brought one, she had no money, not the kind needed to shop at these exclusive stores. To her surprise, he extended his elbow as he'd done at her house and escorted her not into the department store, but the mall entrance.

"My wife had her favorite stores in this mall." Rather than merely browsing, Mitch seemed to have a destination in mind.

As she expected, the place was packed with early holiday shoppers and people of all shapes and sizes. What she hadn't expected was to feel perfectly comfortable on his arm. The other thing that she found surprising was that not a single person seemed to notice him or who he was. As a matter of fact, they walked by person after person and all intent on their tasks didn't seem to notice her either.

Up ahead, a boutique with a small window and only one dress on display caught her eye. Even on a mannequin, the dress was completely mesmerizing. Slowing her steps, she paused to admire how the light shimmered off the flowing skirt. She could only imagine how beautiful it would look on someone like Eve or Paige.

"It's lovely."

She bobbed her head.

Taking a step to one side, he reached for the massive brass door handle. "Shall we go inside? Try it on?"

"No." She shook her head harder than she should have and backing up quickly, almost tripped over her own feet. "I was just looking."

For a second, his brows dipped, either with confusion or concern, probably both since she was reacting as if the dress shop were infested with mice. Just as quickly, a smile replaced the frown. "You sure? We have time."

She stumbled back again. "I'm sure."

"Whatever the lady wants." Closing the distance between them, he waved them forward.

In the distance, bright-colored lights soared to the ceiling. "Oh, look." Again, her steps slowed as they approached the railing center mall. "Isn't it pretty." She just loved the massive tree decked out in holiday fare and the skaters circling around it. "There's something so magical about a Christmas tree. Especially on ice, with all the skaters. Always reminds me of the old Cary Grant holiday movie where he and Loretta Young skated around."

"*The Bishop's Wife.*"

"Yes." She spun around. Not many people still remembered the old black and white movies.

"It's a holiday favorite. As a kid, I always wondered if strangers on the street were really angels."

In her mind's eye, she could see little Mitchell Baron staring up at strangers, looking for an angel. "That's sweet."

"Thank you, because my brothers thought it was lame."

"What do they know?" She smiled, let out a soft sigh at one more glimpse of the tree, and took a step forward.

Walking beside her, he paused. "Do you skate?"

"Are you kidding? I'm lucky I can walk."

Mitch bit back a chuckle. "Come with me."

The next thing she knew, she was sitting on a bench, Mitch kneeling in front of her with her foot in his hand, helping her slip into a scuffed pair of white skates. "I don't think this is a good idea."

He let one foot fall to the padded ground as he lifted the other. "I bet you'll be great. It will be fun."

"I'm not so sure about your definition of fun." Shopping she might have agreed with, but skating, she was far from convinced. Sitting at Mitch's side, she watched with fascination as he laced up in a pair of black skates. "You've done this before."

Leaning over, tying the last lace, he glanced at her. "Played a little recreational hockey as a kid."

Great. She was about to make a bigger idiot of herself on the arm of a man who apparently could do anything he wanted.

"Let's go." He held out his hand and she merely looked down and stared. "I won't bite, but it will be easier on ice if we're holding hands."

Blinking down at how ridiculous she looked in a dress with skates, she accepted the hand and said a small prayer that she wouldn't land on her backside and have to explain to her mother why she came home battered and limping.

One step on the ice and her left foot went forward while her right foot slipped back and only Mitch's tight grip on her hand stopped her from a self-fulfilling prophecy and trip to the ER.

"Maybe," she squeezed his hand a little tighter, "this isn't such a good idea."

Briefly letting go of his hold on her hand, he linked arms and recaptured her hand in his. "You got this. Don't lift your feet, just glide."

"Glide," she repeated to no one in particular. Making an effort not to lift her feet as if walking, she pushed forward.

"See?" He smiled at her and she almost tripped over her own feet. "Now you're getting the hang of it."

Continuing to push one foot in front of the other, it dawned on her that he was right. She wasn't falling. "I'm skating."

Mitch's head tipped back slightly and let out a soft laugh. "You most certainly are. I told you that you'd be great."

Unable to stop the broad grin from spreading across her face, all she could think was what would her mother say if she could see her now?

CHAPTER SIX

Day 2

"So how did it go?" At the ranch, his sister Eve whispered to him while serving bacon at the buffet in the dining room.

"How did what go?" Reaching over her cousin from his other side, Leah Baron grabbed a homemade biscuit.

"Fine and nothing." Surrounded by concerned females, Mitch poured syrup on his pancakes and turned on his heel. His whole reason for taking Gwyneth to the mall was to get a feel for what her taste might be if not ruled by her mother's last century standards. Somehow, once they got there, the idea had seemed rather stupid and instead they wound up skating. He hadn't done that in years and was surprised how much he'd enjoyed it. He was also a bit surprised to discover a sweet, soft-spoken woman who rather than being timid and fearful, seamed surprisingly willing to embrace the unknown. Well, maybe not fully ready to embrace it until she'd realized she wasn't really going to break every bone in her body, but she could have said absolutely not. Instead, she'd carefully tagged along and by the end of the evening, he couldn't get over how radiant Gwyneth looked when she smiled. Really smiled.

With no time left to actually do any window shopping before the mall closed, he'd spent hours late last night and early this morning debating if he should give the shopping idea another try. The other thing that kept kicking around in his head was that beautiful smile. A smile that not only didn't appear often enough, but that was lost in the distraction of an unflattering style.

Sitting across from him, Eve and Leah were deep in

conversation. Either one of them would know exactly what would be involved in bringing Gwyneth into the twenty-first century. The question was, did he want to ask for more help, or more likely, did he have the right?

Another few moments shoveling down his breakfast like a man who hadn't eaten in a week, and something Gwyneth had said in passing played on a never-ending loop in his mind. She would give anything to have even a little bit of Eve's style. *Yep*. That settled it. If Gwyneth was up to it, a trip to the mall was back on his to-do list. Only with Eve in tow. If he could coordinate it.

"I see those wheels turning." His brother Craig sat to his side. His wife was on an out-of-town assignment, so Craig had spent the better part of the week at the ranch. "Washington troubles?"

"No troubles. Just thinking."

"Last I heard, you were having a heck of a time trying to get the backing for the new immigration legislation you'd mapped out. Anyone would think with the whole country in an uproar, someone would finally get on board with a plan. Any plan."

That was where Susan had come in. A tad less conservative than Mitch, she was supposed to be helping garner both his opposition as well as women's votes. Lately she seemed more focused on him than their legislation.

"You still with us?" Fork dangling in midair, Craig stared at his brother.

"Now you've got me thinking about the stalled legislation."

"Sorry. Didn't mean to drag down your morning. So, what were you thinking before I brought up politics?"

"Nothing important. Have some errands to run. Simply sorting through my day."

Craig gave a single dip of his chin. "That's it?"

Some would consider all the questions an unwelcome imposition. Although Mitch was a grown man with no need of supervision, the fact that all the brothers kept an eye out for his siblings, including asking questions that might not be any of their business, was endearing. "That's it."

Reluctantly, Craig nodded, and dropped his napkin on the table. "If you say so, but I have to run. I'm expecting a delivery at the studio and want to follow up on it personally."

"See you later." Mitch gestured to his brother's departing back only to have his sister slip into Craig's vacated seat.

"Did you get a chance to chat with Gwyneth?"

He nodded.

"And?"

"No and."

Eve shook her head. "Why are men so obtuse sometimes?"

What the heck was obtuse about not wanting to kiss and tell, even if there was no actual kissing involved.

"Are you still going with her to the gala?"

Again he nodded and before his sister could roll her eyes at him again and make some other disparaging remark about his gender, he figured now was as good a time as any to speak up. "I realized after talking with her last night at the mall—"

"You went to the mall?"

"Yes." He waved her off. "But that's not important. I realized that she is very much aware of how she stands out in a crowd and it is very much fueling her awkwardness. I believe she would embrace a chance to, uh, modernize."

Eve raised one brow, but said nothing.

"I'm no Pygmalion. Would you be willing to help?"

It took Eve a long minute of staring at him before she finally nodded. "I'm not Professor Higgins either, but if the butterfly wants out of the cocoon, I'm all for helping."

That he was glad to hear. Despite everything, somehow he knew deep down a butterfly had to be hidden inside Gwyneth Van Klein.

"Really, Gwyneth." Her mother huffed from her seat at the

head of the nearly empty dinner table. The thing was built to accommodate her parents and her three brothers as well as herself and guests. Her mother looked a tad lost behind the massive oak piece. "Coming in after ten o'clock last night. And un-chaperoned."

That was almost enough to make Gwyneth laugh. Like any man would have enough interest in her to require the need of a chaperone.

"And please explain to me since when you have been so friendly with Mitchell Baron?"

"We've known each other for ages, Mother. You know that." After all, it was her mother and Lila Baron who had arranged for Mitch to accompany Gwyneth at her coming-out party when the candidate her mother had chosen backed out at the last minute.

"I know perfectly well how long our family has been friends with Lila's family."

An interesting choice of words. Not the Baron family, but Lila's. As if the Governor had nothing to do with it. Though she was sure her mother would be more approving of Mitchell and his siblings if their grandfather's pedigree had been as old and pristine as Lila Conroe Baron's.

"Excuse me, Miss Gwyneth." Oliver, the family butler, appeared in the doorway. "You have a call. Senator Baron."

Her mother's eyes narrowed and Gwyneth had to work hard not to spring up out of her seat like a cat chasing a mouse. "I'll take it in the study."

"Really, I don't see—"

Gwyneth was out of the room and locking the study door behind her before her mother could finish her sentence. "Hello."

"Good morning. I'm sorry to call so early, but I was wondering if you had some free time this morning to finish what we started yesterday?"

"More skating?" After all, that was all they'd done.

A deep chuckle seeped through the phone and she found herself needing to sit. "No, I meant the window shopping. My sister Eve was hoping to tag along, if you're free?"

If she was free. Time was one thing she had plenty of.

Always. "What time were you thinking?"

"Oh, in about an hour?"

Good, she thought. If he'd said this afternoon, she didn't think she'd be able to handle her mother harping at her for hours about Mitchell Baron. "That will be perfect. I'll be waiting."

"Good. See you soon."

Staring a few moments at the phone in the cradle, she sucked in a breath and decided an escape to her room was in order. Not that there was much she could do to make herself more presentable, but at least it would mitigate her mother's third degree.

In her room she considered brushing her hair, but it would only wind up in a bun at the back of her head again. Staring into her closet, she searched for something not quite so matronly and then closed the door. There was no such thing in her closet and she knew it. Many a time she'd considered taking some of her meager savings to buy a nice dress online, but what was the point? Not only did she not have anywhere to wear it—especially not without her mother noticing—lipstick on a pig is still a pig.

A rap at the door had her jumping in her seat.

"Miss. The Senator is here."

Thank heaven she'd avoided her mother. Another few minutes and she'd made it out the door and into Mitch's car, her mother never leaving the parlor.

"Glad you could come." Mitch drove past the gates of the Van Klein estate.

Gwyneth smiled. She feared if she opened her mouth to say anything, she'd be gushing her gratitude for an even brief escape from her normal world.

"So happy you don't mind me tagging along." Like a little kid, Eve leaned forward between the bucket seats. "I just love shopping."

Shopping? Gwyneth held back a wave of unease. She didn't have money to shop. Mitch had said window shopping, surely that's what Eve meant. For the remainder of the ride to the mall, Eve chattered at Gwyneth as if they'd been life long friends. Every so often Gwyneth felt obliged to nod and recognize that she was part of the conversation, but for the most part, Eve did fine by herself.

"I thought we'd start here." Eve waved a finger at the large department store as her brother pulled into a parking spot. "Get a feel for what looks best on you."

"On me?" Now Gwyneth could feel her throat tightening. Did they actually expect her to try clothes on?

"Well," Eve smiled, "I might be in the market for something new too."

And that pushed the air back into her lungs. Shopping for Eve, she could handle.

"Ms. Baron." A slim blonde who looked to have fallen out of a page of *Women's Wear Daily* greeted Eve with a huge smile.

"So glad you had time to help."

"For you there's always time." The blonde moved forward. "I've set up a private dressing room, and based on our conversation, pulled a few things for you and Ms. Van Klein to try."

"I suppose this is time for me to go hunting a cup of coffee." Mitch smiled.

"Not on your life." Eve looped her arm with her brother's. "They have wonderfully comfortable chairs for big brothers to sit in and wait for the fashion show."

Fashion show. The air in Gwyneth's lungs threatened to choke her.

"If you'd like, Senator." The blonde smiled at Mitch. "I'll have the café bring you some coffee."

He nodded. "That would be nice. Thank you."

The next thing Gwyneth knew she was standing in a dressing room almost the size of her own room, stripped down to her underwear and staring at a sleek midnight blue gown.

"Let me help." Eve held the gown from the hanger and slowly unzipped it. "I just want an idea of what styles go with your figure."

She had a figure? She had hips that wouldn't quit and doubted she'd get one thigh into that dress, never mind two.

Glancing over at her, Eve narrowed her gaze, then

shook her head. "Let's start with this one instead." The woman probably noticed the extra pounds Gwyneth's normal wardrobe disguised.

Taking hold of the hanger and dress, she wondered if she was supposed to pull it over her head or step into it. Several awkward seconds spent staring at the gown passed, when Eve easily slipped out of her outfit and slid her own gown over her head. Of course. Stepping into a gown would run the risk of tearing something. The only problem, once she had the dress on, she looked like a kid playing dress up. Nothing fit the way it should. Who was she kidding?

Eve spun about. "Zip this for me, please."

"Of course." She pulled up the zipper and no surprise, Eve looked amazing.

"Here. Let me get yours."

Gwyneth shook her head. "It won't help." She began pulling her arms out of the short sleeves.

"Give it a minute." Eve stepped over and insisted on zipping her up. The dress wasn't quite form-fitting and shot out from her knees at an awkward angle, but Eve had been correct, it didn't look quite as bad zipped. Not good, but not as bad.

Shaking her head, Eve's mouth twisted in thought. "You're right. Not your style."

If Eve thought she was going to find something to make her look stylish, she was down right delusional.

"Let's try this one."

Once again she stripped down to her sensible cotton underwear and wished she owned something lacey and pretty like Eve wore, but her mother didn't believe in frilly underthings, the same way she didn't believe in dieting, salacious romance books, strappy insensible shoes, and hard liquor.

"Now we're talking." Eve stood smiling at her.

She spun around and dared to look in the mirror. Eve was right. This dress wasn't as off-putting, but no matter how she sliced it, she still looked like a grandmother in a Barbie dress. Why did she even bother?

CHAPTER SEVEN

Day 3

Sitting behind the desk of his grandfather's study, Mitch did his best to catch up on work emails. The task was proving difficult. No matter what the email content, his mind kept wandering back to yesterday and shopping with Gwyneth. Every once in a while, her eyes would light up, something a kin to a child seeing a Fourth of July fireworks or the lighting of the town Christmas tree.

He would have liked to have done more shopping, find things that would keep that delighted glint in her eyes, but he and his sister had agreed not to be gone too long as that might stir suspicion or ire or who knew what unpleasantness from Prudence. They'd stopped at trying on only a few dresses. The problem, as Eve put it, was the work that would have to go along with the dress. Simply buying a new gown was not the answer to making Gwyneth feel like she fit in.

As his sister ran through the list of people who would need to be available on the day of the gala to primp, trim, and prep Gwyneth, was mind-boggling to him. All he needed was a quick shave and shower and he was good to go. His sister had reassured him that she could handle all the accessories without needing Gwyneth nearby, except maybe the shoes. And of course, a decision would have to be made about the dress. It had become evident rather quickly that much of Gwyneth's reticence with all the talk of shopping was that her mother controlled the purse strings. Just thinking about it had him fuming. Even a child received an allowance, never mind a full-grown woman.

"Knock knock." Eve stood in the doorway. "Busy?"

"I should be." Mitch tossed the pen he'd been fidgeting with onto the desk. "What's on your mind?"

"Probably the same thing on yours."

He refrained from vocalizing Gwyneth's name.

"I think I may have figured out a way around a few things."

"I'm all ears." He leaned forward, listening with interest to Eve's scheming to get Gwyneth away from Prudence for all they needed to do. His sister was an amazing and smart woman, and right about now, he admired every inch of her sneaky mind.

"So what do you think?" Eve asked from the chair in front of the desk.

"Have you run this past Grams and the others?"

She nodded.

"They're on board?"

"Everyone loves a Cinderella story."

Cinderella. Prudence certainly had the cutting mother role down pat. What he wanted to know was, where was a good fairy godmother when you needed one?

All through breakfast Gwyneth sat quietly listening to her mother's lectures. If there had been any doubt in her mind that her mother had intended to set a match for her and Reginald Livingston, it was completely gone now.

She could still hear her mother's superior tone. "I have it on good authority that Reginald regrets deeply that his wife could not bear children. With no other relatives, he wants to have a child. Of course, no ordinary wife would do. To bear him a son he needs a woman with good breeding, good genes, and a strong family history of producing sons. The Van Kleins and the Livingstons would create a near-perfect bloodline."

For the remainder of the conversation, she felt like a brood mare. One to be quickly discarded if she couldn't produce the next Triple Crown winner. There was no sense in pointing out to her mother that having three brothers did not improve her chances of bearing sons for Reginald or anyone else. There was also no way to ask why her mother, after all these years, had suddenly developed an interest in marrying off the daughter who until now she'd been perfectly content keeping home at her side. The child who was supposed to return her mother's loving affections by caring for her in her declining years. Loving affections. Had Prudence Van Klein ever really loved anyone?

"I will not live forever and a well-suited marriage would secure your future. Your brothers are established in their own right and there is no doubt of their future."

"Why is that, Mother? Why did Father not leave a trust for me as with my brothers?" She almost slapped her hand over her mouth, surprised at her own nerve to ask the question that had haunted her for years.

Prudence Van Klein lifted her tea cup but didn't sip. "Because knowing what a strong-willed small child you were, your father wisely left your care and education to me. To ensure when the time came you would make all the right choices."

Like Reginald, she shuddered.

"The right choice includes the right match. Not a mongrel like the Barons."

"The Barons have an excellent family history."

Swallowing a sip, her mother set the tea cup in the saucer. "Lila Conroe's family can be traced back as far as ours. But the Governor is nothing but a street mutt. Now, Reginald's family can be traced back to every page of the Boston Social Register. Barons make excellent friends, but don't delude yourself into thinking there can be anything more. You'll keep your promise to attend the gala and then you will focus on Reginald."

If she heard her mother go on again about the importance of strong bloodlines for good breeding, she might throw up.

Nothing was as much of a relief as when Oliver entered the room, interrupting her mother's soap box. "A call for Miss Gwyneth from Mrs. Lila Baron."

"Lila? For Gwyneth? Did she say what it was in reference to?"

"No, ma'am."

"Very well." Her mother waved her away with her fingers. "Hurry up, child. Don't leave Lila waiting."

Without a nod or response, Gwyneth left the parlor and took the call.

"Hello Gwyneth. I hope today finds you well?" Lila Baron's smiling voice came across the line.

"Yes, ma'am. How may I help you?"

"It appears I'm playing interference. Please hold the line."

"Good morning." Two simple words in a now familiar deep timbre had her smiling. "I have something I need to do today and thought it would be nice if you joined me. This way we can go over a few things about the gala as well, but we thought it best not to alert your mother."

"Of course."

"Can I pick you up?"

"Yes. That will be fine." It didn't matter where they went or what he wanted to talk about. Anything with Mitch would be better than sitting home alone carving her boxes or hiding out to read one of those insensible romances her mother deplored.

"Wonderful. My grandmother is going to call your mother and thank her for allowing you to help her with a little project. Then I'll be there shortly to pick you up. Oh, and wear sensible shoes for walking outdoors."

As if she owned anything other than sensible shoes. "Outdoors?"

"That's what I said." She could hear the humor in his voice. Could it be that after only a couple of days spent together, she was learning to read the moods and tones of Mitchell Baron? "Sensible as in flat and laced."

She could do that. "I'll be ready." For what, she had no idea, but she very much wanted to be something.

✭

If there was one thing Mitch was sure of, it was that he needed to get Gwyneth away from the prying eyes and ears of Prudence Van Klein, and killing two birds with one stone seemed to be the easiest way. As usual, Oliver opened the front door with a blank expression. The man would have been a marvelous guard at Buckingham Palace.

"Morning, Oliver. Mrs. Baron asked me to pick up Miss Gwyneth."

"Yes, sir. Miss Gwyneth is expecting you."

"Miss Gwyneth is ready." To his surprise she stood in the foyer wearing a pair of black slacks, a matching shirt and sweater, and, of course, very sensible shoes.

"Shall we?" He extended his elbow to her. The hesitancy in her reaction almost had him wondering if she thought his arm would bite. Once they were in the car and the door to the house had closed behind them, he put the car in gear.

"Where are we going?"

"To the ranch."

"Do my shoes have anything to do with your grandmother's project?"

"Sort of. My grandmother has given me a task and I thought you could help me."

Her gaze narrowed before she sucked in a long, slow breath. "I should warn you, my skill sets are limited."

"All you need is a good eye."

"As long as I'm wearing my glasses." Hands clasped in her lap, her insecurities came over in waves.

He wanted to bite his tongue for mentioning a good eye, or anything else that would add to her unease. "Do you really want to know what we're doing?"

Lips pressed tightly closed, she nodded.

"Every year in preparation for Christmas, my grandparents have people who come in and decorate the house from top to bottom, inside and out."

"So does Mother. At least, she used to until we moved Christmas dinner to my brother Calvin's home."

"Paradise Ridge looks like the North Pole every year, except one tree. The tree in the smaller family room is always cut down by one of us and then decorated over the weekend by the family."

"Really?" She smiled. "That sounds lovely."

"Glad you think so, because this year I've been tasked with picking the tree. Grams likes to have one tree all set up by the family before the pros come in for the rest of the house. Everyone else is busy this week, not even my sisters can help, so this is where you come in. Lots of pressure finding the perfect tree."

"Me?" Her eyes rounded and he knew he wasn't doing anything to calm her nerves.

Some days he wanted to just throttle Prudence Van Klein for robbing her daughter of any self-esteem or confidence. "Relax. It will be fun. You'll see."

She bobbed her head unconvincingly and didn't say another word until he parked the car at the ranch by the barn.

"I just need a second." He waved a finger at her, trotted inside and came out with a chainsaw. "We'll take a four-wheeler."

"You're really going to cut it down yourself?" The incredulity in her gaze had him biting back a chuckle.

"Yep. Come on."

Hands at her side, she hurried to keep up and climbed into the four-wheeler.

"Buckle in."

She nodded. Frowning down at the seat belt, she fumbled with the latches, not quite snapping it in place.

"Let me." He reached over her, untwisted the shoulder strap, then pulled it loosely across her. For just a second, he could see the panic in her eyes as her gaze followed his hands. The look of a trapped animal had his own heart racing and his anger with Prudence Van Klein brewing again. So much for keeping Gwyneth at ease to discuss Eve's plan.

It took two tugs to get the difficult latch to click in place. Lifting his gaze to meet hers, he momentarily froze. Not till now had he noticed how long dark lashes shadowed sparkling gray-blue eyes, and her complexion seemed to shout Peaches and Cream.

"Is… is it broken?"

Her words snapped him back to the task at hand. Tearing his gaze away and refocusing on the seat belt, he heard the click as the safety belt snapped into place. "Just stuck."

He pushed himself back into his seat and started the ignition. Bouncing down the rolling hills of Paradise Ridge, he did his best to slow his racing heart, reminding himself he had always been, and always would be, in love with Abbie. A man only got one chance in a lifetime for love and he'd had his. Right now, he was just anxious because Gwyneth was ill at ease. None of what he was feeling now had a thing to do with those deep blue eyes, luscious eyelashes, or blushing cheek bones. Nothing at all.

CHAPTER EIGHT

For a full thirty seconds, Gwyneth thought she might actually have stopped breathing. Having Mitch's arms and hands and warm breath so close to her ignited a plethora of sensations she didn't have a clue how to begin dealing with.

"We should be there in a few minutes." He flashed her what was no doubt intended to be a reassuring smile. All it did was make her stomach do a somersault.

Another few minutes of bumpy silence and a crop of thick green pine trees drew closer. "It looks like a movie."

"The Governor planted the grove when he and Grams were first married. With every tree that comes down, another one gets planted. It took a while to find the species that could thrive in Houston's climate, but every year we cut down one of our own."

"I've never cut down a Christmas tree before." She'd never decorated one either. If she were honest, Christmas was one of her least favorite days of the year. The stress of appropriate gifts and appropriate reactions to being given something you couldn't stand was more than she could handle some years.

"Cutting is the easy part, picking it out is the hard one. Grams is very particular. It has to be just perfect."

And again, the stress of the season that until today hadn't quite descended on her had just arrived with a vengeance.

"Okay." The vehicle came to a stop and turning the key off, he hopped out. "Ready?"

No was probably not the answer he wanted. Instead she nodded and climbed out.

"We'll start on this side where the more mature trees are. Then we'll work our way through until one looks right."

"Okay." She took two steps forward, slipped in a divot and before she could catch her own balance, Mitch's arms looped around her.

"Careful."

Once again, he was up close and personal and Gwyneth had never been more confused in her life. "Sorry."

Sure she was steady on her feet, he took a short step back. "That's why I requested sensible shoes."

"Good call." She hoped her smile looked more sure than she felt. Glancing at the pines surrounding them, she studied the one in front of her more closely. "Exactly what does your grandmother want in a tree? Besides perfection."

Mitch chuckled. "Solid triangular shape. She doesn't like them too thick or too thin and she hates bald spots."

"Not too thin, not too fat, and not too bald. Got it."

His soft chuckle grew to a heartfelt laugh. "Yep." He stopped and pointed to the tree to his left. "How about this one?"

Squinting, she found herself leaning left, her gaze following the growth of the tree. "Too crooked."

Lifting his gaze to the top of the tree, he frowned then nodded. "Yeah. You're right." Mitch marched forward, glancing at a tree or two as he advanced.

Slightly ahead, a tree caught her eye. From here it looked to fit all the criteria. She'd have to get closer for a final evaluation.

"This one looks good." Pointing at the tree beside him, he began waving his arm between the branches. "Not too thick, not too thin."

Taking her time to walk around, she shook her head. "Bald spot here, and here, and—"

"Never mind." He smiled. "We'll keep looking."

When they reached the one she'd had her eye on, she took her time walking around it, then lifted her gaze to the top. Content that it was indeed close to perfect, she waved an arm at it. "How about this one?"

Mitch came to a stop about six feet away, looked up, then down, and very slowly the corners of his mouth tipped up until he sported a full-blown smile. "You found it."

Looking to her right at the tree, she smiled equally wide. She had indeed.

Pride at finding the perfect tree lit up Gwyneth's face. This had to be her brightest smile yet, and Mitch was quickly discovering that he liked seeing it.

In agreement that this was indeed *the* tree, he pulled out the chainsaw and quickly cut the pine down from the base.

"I hope it's not too big." Gwyneth frowned at the tree sprawled across the ground.

Mitch shook his head. "If it is, it won't be the first or last time our eyes were bigger than our living room." As he'd hoped, the quip brought the smile back to Gwyneth's face. "We'll just nip a bit more off the bottom."

She bobbed her head. "Makes sense."

"In the spring, we'll come out and plant another seedling in this spot. In ten years or so, this might be another contender."

"How long has your family had this tradition?" Gwyneth stood to one side as he slung twine around the tree branches, making it easier to transport.

"I honestly don't know." He pushed to his feet and stood the tree on end. "For as long as I can remember. I'm pretty sure they've done this since my dad and his siblings were young."

Together, they hefted the tree up and onto the back of the four-wheeler. Both ends hung far over the sides.

As she climbed into the front seat, Gwyneth shook her head. "I don't know about this."

"It will be fine. You'll see."

At the house, the two of them lifted the massive, and heavy, tree off the vehicle and onto the back veranda.

"I need to put the four-wheeler away and then we can

come back and set this thing up in the den."

"Do you need me to stay with the tree?"

He shook his head. "Nope. It'll still be here when we get back. We'll only be a few minutes."

Gwyneth quickly climbed back into the four-wheeler. He simply loved that she was moving about with much less hesitancy. In only a few days she seemed to be acquiring, or perhaps just getting a chance to practice at exploring some self-confidence.

"Mack is probably gone for the day. I just need to park this inside." He drove all the way into the vehicle barn and turned off the ignition.

"What's that?" Hopping off the vehicle, Gwyneth walked toward his pet project.

"It will be a plane."

She spun around. "Will be?"

"I've been working on it here and there in my spare time for the last few years. Something to keep my mind busy since, well…to keep my hands busy too."

"You're building this yourself?" Gwyneth walked past the project and slowly stretching her arm out, ran her hand along the side of one wing. "Wow. I'm impressed."

Why those three words made him want to puff out his chest and strut like a peacock, he didn't know. "It's actually my second effort. The first one I got in too deep too quick with not enough knowledge of aeronautical mathematics."

"But it's going well now?"

He nodded. "Bought this from a popular kit company. They make and sell more home-built airplanes than anyone else in the world. Makes it easier for us to put together."

"There's a good reason more home-built planes are churned out than all major manufactures in the world put together."

"That's right." Odd thing for her to know.

"So you're doing this alone?"

"Mostly. A couple of things I brought Cooper in to make sure I didn't muck it up."

"Helps having an engineer in the family."

"It helps having a little bit of everything in the family."

She continued to walk around the plane. "Planning a trip to Alaska?"

"Excuse me?"

"This is a bush plane. Right?"

"Yes. It is." He chuckled. She might know more about planes than he did. "But the only place I hope to go is up."

"Who's going to fly it?"

"Me."

Stopping suddenly, she looked over her shoulder at him. "You're a pilot?"

He shrugged. "That's what my license says. My family don't all quite agree."

"Really?" She continued walking. "I've read that these kits don't even come with plans anymore."

"Correct."

"The parts are beautifully fabricated on CNC machines. They say it's not really building, it's almost like playing with tinker toys, but doesn't look that way to me"

How did she keep so much miscellaneous information in her mind? "That might be a smidge of an exaggeration. Maybe more like assembling Ikea furniture."

"Perhaps, but it is beautiful."

"Thank you. Aviation has come a long way. These aircrafts are modern, sophisticated, and better built than a factory."

"I can see that." Her attention remained completely focused on his pet project. "It must be amazing to build something so useful with your own hands."

"We'll see if I finish."

"*When* you finish." She hadn't even looked up at him when she said that. He'd missed having someone who believed unwaveringly in him. Of course he came from a family that always had his back, but it wasn't the same as having one person to faithfully cheer him on.

"When." He corrected himself with a smile. At first the plane had been one of the key things to keep him sane while missing Abbie. Now he seemed to be spending less and less time on the project. Maybe he should get back to it. "Do you like to fly?"

"Don't know."

"You've never been in a small plane?"

"I've never been on any plane."

That stopped him cold. Prudence Van Klein could not have done a better job of stifling a delightful human being if she'd had a full-time staff to assist. "Would you like to go for a ride when it's finished?"

Her gaze lifted to meet his and a flash of something he had yet to see flickered in her eyes. "Yes. I believe…I believe I would."

"What are you girls looking at now?" Lila Baron put down her knitting and pushing to her feet, walked to the window, Honey and Moon at her heels.

A curtain in hand, holding it away from the window, her granddaughters Eve, Siobhan, and Rachel stood looking outside.

Lila stood behind them, peering over their shoulders. "I don't see anything worth standing here all afternoon for."

"It's Mitch," Rachel said softly, followed by Siobhan's, "and Gwyneth. They're in the barn. Still."

"Yes." Lila acknowledged. Siobhan had arrived from her and Jack's visit to her mother's, and already was all caught up in the Gwyneth and Mitch news. "They're cutting down the tree today."

Rachel spun around to face her grandmother. "But picking the tree is almost as much fun as decorating."

"I know," Lila said.

Staring back out the window, Rachel turned to her cousins. "Did y'all know Mitch was cutting down a tree today without any of us?"

Siobhan shrugged, and Eve nodded. "Seemed right."

"Right?" Rachel looked sideways at Eve then turned to her grandmother. "What am I missing here?"

"Gwyneth." Lila sighed. She'd known for a very long time that Prudence was an overbearing, stifling mother, but she also knew that Gwyneth was smart and astute and hoped some day she'd find the strength to stand up for herself. This most recent plan of Prudence's was the last straw for Lila. She simply couldn't stand by silently any longer.

"We've decided that someone needs to help Gwyneth blossom." Eve continued to stare out the window.

"Blossom? What is she, a tulip?" Rachel returned her gaze out the window.

"I like to think of her as a rose, waiting for a fresh rain to bloom." When her granddaughters glanced over their shoulders at her, Lila shrugged. "So, I'm not a poet."

The three women actually giggled like schoolgirls.

Eve turned to her cousin. "What Grams means is that we're hoping to turn the ugly duckling into a swan. The challenge is we've only got a short while to help her grow a backbone first."

"Correct," Lila agreed. "Otherwise her mother will just squash our well-intentioned efforts."

Rachel frowned, staring out the window and then turned. "So, what you're saying is y'all are her fairy godmothers—of sorts?"

"Leah's in on it too." Eve nodded.

A smile tipped at the corners of Rachel's mouth. "I don't know what the plan is, and a person isn't the same thing as a house, but you gotta know, if we're making sure that Gwyneth Van Klein shines in all her glory, I want in!"

"Oh look," Siobhan pointed outside, "here they come. She does look more relaxed. I think spending time away from Prudence—"

"And accomplishing things for herself," Lila interrupted.

"Right," Eve agreed. "I think it's helping build her self-confidence."

"Which," Rachel said, "explains why you wanted the two of them picking out the perfect tree without a dozen bickering cousins tagging along."

"Exactly." Lila smiled.

Stepping away from the window, Eve rubbed her hands enthusiastically. "I say tomorrow we hit the stores again.

Accessory time."

"I love shopping. I'm in." Rachel nodded.

"Not me." Siobhan sighed. "I have a shoot for *Texas Digest*. I'll be out of town till the weekend of the gala, but I know y'all can handle this."

Lila smiled to herself. Her granddaughters were truly kindhearted souls. "I'll call Prudence tomorrow and let her know we'll be picking Gwyneth up again."

"Again?" Rachel stepped away from the window.

"We were afraid Prudence would smell a rat if Mitch keeps whisking Gwyneth away." Lila shrugged. "So I told Prudence that my girls are terribly busy with Eve and Paige married now, and Siobhan's career booming that I could use some help with the gala from Gwyneth. I simply neglected to mention that Gwyneth is the project we're all working on."

Rachel stood on her toes and kissed her grandmother's cheek. "I love a good sneak."

"We aim to please." Lila rolled onto her heels and smiled at her granddaughters. She just hoped in the end Prudence didn't take a hammer to the carefully built house of cards.

CHAPTER NINE

Gwyneth resisted the urge to pinch herself. Cutting down a Christmas tree yesterday afternoon with Mitch and then visiting with his sisters and cousin afterward had been one of the nicest times she'd had since, well, since skating with Mitch the other night. Rather than finding him to be a stern, imposing man always ready to wield his power like her elder brothers, he had proven to be sweet and charming, exactly how she remembered him from all those years ago, and—the icing on the cake— surprisingly easy to talk to.

Still high on the good mood she'd enjoyed, she'd curled up in bed, trying to read a much anticipated novel. Instead of getting lost in the prose, she found her mind wandering back to snippets of time spent with Mitch. More startling was her imagination's tendency to circle round to a life and home with a man like Mitch. A man who was merely being kind and helpful. She would have to remind herself of that over and over again until after the gala. Once their single public appearance together was over, life would return to the isolated world she'd been accustomed to.

Now, after Lila once again had sent for her, she sat watching a plethora of Barons laughing and teasing and delighting in one ornament after the other. If there had ever been this kind of joy and happiness in her family home, she had no memory of it.

"I know it's not cold out," Mitch sat on the loveseat beside her, "but Hazel makes the absolute best hot cocoa on the planet. You have to have at least one."

"Thank you." The mug in front of her, smothered in tiny marshmallows and whipped cream, smelled divine.

"You seem deep in thought." Mitch leaned back and crossing one ankle over his knee, took a slow sip of his own warm brew.

Still blowing on her cocoa, she couldn't stop the chuckle that escaped.

"Something funny?"

She bobbed her head. "You now have a chocolate and whipped cream mustache."

"Oh." His eyes popped open and he sprang forward in his seat, set the cup on the table, and pulled out a handkerchief from his pocket.

"I gather this is the other reason your grandparents insisted you keep a drawer full of hankies."

Wiping his mouth, he folded the cloth, slipped it back into his pocket, and nodded. "That would be an affirmative. I just didn't expect to need it twice in one week."

She tried to keep the smile on her face. She so hated that he'd seen her crying on the veranda that day, and yet, if he hadn't, she wouldn't be here now.

"So," he leaned back again, "what deep thoughts are you simmering over?"

No way was she ready to share her daydreams. "Nothing really."

His phone dinged at his side and he quickly swiped at it. Another moment ticked by and his phone dinged again, and again he rejected the call.

"Do you get a lot of scam calls?"

"Not really. One perk of Congress is a truly non-accessible cell phone number."

Cradling her mug in her hands, she tipped her head to one side. She'd become very good at recognizing evasion tactics. "Of course. So you're just being polite ignoring texts while talking to someone?"

The way one brow lifted higher than the other, she was pretty sure he caught the incredulity in her tone of voice. "You noticed."

"Kind of hard to miss. Want to talk about it?"

From the way he was twirling his wedding ring, sliding it up and down his knuckle, she suspected he was dodging more than just phone calls. His gaze shifted to the phone on the table beside him. Blowing out a soft sigh, he shoved the ring down hard on his finger and shifted to face her. "I've been trying for over a year to garner support for an immigration bill. What some of us consider a sensible way to deal with the need for manual labor in this country."

"I've always thought it absurd that immigration policies have been non-existent since the sixties."

He stared at her for a moment. "You're referring to the end of Ellis Island and entry to all?"

This time she nodded. "We're supposed to learn from history. Every generation has depended upon immigrants to fill the needs of service industries. Without a policy in place to allow for legal immigration to fill not only positions Americans *cannot* do, but do not *want* to do, we're going to remain in a vicious cycle."

"Exactly." He smiled at her. "But trying to get both sides of the aisle onboard has been difficult. I've been working on this for a couple of years now with another senator, but her focus has been shifting more and more and I haven't figured out how to extricate myself from an awkward situation—"

"Without making enemies and burning bridges," she interrupted.

"I'm sorry. Were you in politics once upon a time and I missed it?" he teased.

"Hardly. But I do read a great deal. Can you tell me more?"

Without hesitating, he twisted to better face her and began explaining his plans for the border crisis, the labor issues, and creating a more practical and feasible immigration policy. Not only was the man incredibly handsome, kind, and thoughtful, he didn't need to rest on his family pedigree—even if her mother considered him a mongrel—his ideas were fully able to stand on their own merit. That is if he could convince enough members of Congress to get off their special interest derrieres and actually look at the problem, and one part of the solution.

"So you see why I need Susan's help, but I fear there's

no easy way out of the mess I seem to have created."

"Mm," she muttered. No one would blame the female senator for being interested in Mitch for more than his legislation. At the moment, she wished she had a good answer for him. Wished she could wave a magic wand and make everything fall into place. "This isn't helpful, but I have faith you'll find the way."

"Glad someone does." He laughed at himself and let his foot fall to the floor. "I shouldn't have bothered you with any of this."

"It's no bother. Have you talked to your family about this? Do they have a suggestion?"

He shook his head. "You're the only one I've told."

The only one? He actually trusted her with his troubles. Had anyone in her family ever cared for her opinion? Trusted her thoughts? Her heart stuttered and her breath hitched. Now more than ever, she wanted to find answers, to help, to be worthy of his trust. When no one else would agree to escort her to the coming-out ball her mother had painstakingly thrown to purposely outdo every socialite on the planet, Mitch had not only stepped up to save her day merely because his grandmother had asked him to, he'd done his best to see that shy, tongue-tied her had a good time. Though it may not have seemed that way to anyone else, she'd had the best time of her life. Somewhere there had to be an answer to his dilemma, if only she could actually come up with something to help.

Leaning back again, he heaved a heavy sigh. "When Abbie was alive, I'd bounce things like this off of her. She had great instincts and better insight."

"No wonder you still miss her."

His gaze lifted to meet hers. "I do. But not as often as I used to."

"They say time heals all wounds. A bit of a cliché, but there's probably at least a grain of truth to it. If not heals, at least teaches us how to live with them."

Gently, he let his hand rest on her arm. "Thank you for listening."

She swallowed hard and nodded. "Any time."

Why had Mitch burdened Gwyneth with his troubles? Today was supposed to be another step to building her self-confidence and self-esteem. To equip her with better tools to stand up to her mother, to help her become the woman he knew she was deep inside. Instead, here he was looking for support and maybe even answers.

"And why are you two just sitting there?" Rachel stood with her hands on her hips. "There's tinsel to be hung still."

"Oh, no." He couldn't stop himself from whining just a bit. "Grams is so much better at it than I am. The tree looks magical when she does the tinsel. It looks like a tornado blew through when I do it."

"You know the secret." Rachel glared at him.

He blew out a frustrated sigh. "One strand at a time. It takes forever that way."

"It's the only way to not look—as you so eloquently put it—like a tornado blew through. Come on." Tugging on his hand, she let go when he came to his feet.

"If I'm doing this, so are you." He extended his hand to Gwyneth, surprised when their fingertips sparked. "Must be the carpet."

She nodded and came to her feet, kindly failing to point out they were standing on hardwood floors. "No promises to not look like a tornado blew through."

"That's the spirit!" Rachel smiled and turned toward the hall.

"Hey," Mitch called after her. "Aren't you going to hang tinsel?"

His cousin tipped her chin up and flashed a toothy grin. "Not on your life. Siobhan's making her mother's famous eggnog and I promised to help." Laughing loudly, she exited the room, her laughter lingering as she made her way down the hall to meet up with her cousin.

"Women."

"I beg your pardon." Eve appeared out of nowhere.

"Sorry." He leaned forward and kissed his sister on the

cheek. "No offense intended."

"Well, since you apologized so nicely. I'll forgive you. Just this once." She waved a finger at him then turned to Gwyneth. "While I have you almost alone, a few of us are going to do a little accessory shopping one day this week. I thought it might be a fun girls' outing if you joined us."

"Me?"

Eve looked left and right, her gaze settling on Mitch. "Certainly not him."

"Oh. Well. Uhm. Yes, I think I can do that."

"Don't worry." His sister let her hand come to rest on Gwyneth's arm. "I'll have Grams call and clear the way. No one says *no* to Grams."

"Thank you." She seemed to relax. "I'd love to."

"Good." As Eve turned, she casually winked at him. Though Gwyneth didn't know it—yet—operation Save Gwyneth was clearly in full force. He could hardly wait to see how they were going to pull it all off with so little time left.

"Where are my tinsel people?" His grandmother stood by an open box of tinsel packets.

"Here." Mitch waved at her, bringing Gwyneth with him. Not till he reached his grandmother's side and her gaze dropped to their clasped hands did he realize that he was even holding it. Trying not to look like he'd grabbed hold of a live wire, he casually released his grip and reached into the big box with two hands, giving one package to Gwyneth and ripping another open with his teeth.

"Really, Mitchell. We have scissors." His grandmother sighed ever so gently and twisting in place, grabbed a nearby pair of scissors and handed them to Gwyneth. "Here you go, before my grandson the senator chews at your packet too."

"Thank you." Gwyneth smiled. "I understand there's a trick to it."

Grams nodded and sliding a handful of tinsel over her hand, showed Gwyneth how to gently place the strands. Turning her head left then right, she leaned into Gwyneth and whispered, "It's really two or three strands at a time, but if you tell these galoots that, they'll drop the whole clump on it."

Mitch wasn't supposed to hear the older woman's advice, but he did. And more importantly, he saw Gwyneth's sweet smile break open at his grandmother's secret. Gwyneth really did have a lovely smile. He couldn't help but wonder what might have been different all those years ago, the one and only time he was her escort, had Gwyneth Van Klein been born into any other family that let her personality shine?

CHAPTER TEN

After spending a few days back to back with Mitch and the Barons, the last couple of days at her own home had felt especially empty for Gwyneth. She'd never found her house anything special, or even warm and friendly, but suddenly it felt downright stark and cold. More than once, she'd considered calling Mitch to simply check up on how his plans for the new legislation were going, but never found the nerve to actually pick up the phone.

When Eve called last night to ask if she was free to join them shopping today, Gwyneth was thrilled. When the invitation included supper with the family at the ranch afterward, including Mitch, she almost did a jig in place.

She hadn't said a word the day they'd tried on dresses, but it had been years since her mother had taken her out to an actual shop. All of her dresses were now custom made to her mother's standards from a dressmaker's form of her figure. Once she'd gotten over the shock of dressing and undressing in front of Eve and her cousins, she'd actually enjoyed the day, but today was a whole new learning curve.

The first thing to surprise her was when the saleswoman came out with a tray of red and white wine. Did people actually shop and drink at the same time? She tried on sandals, summer heels, dress shoes, and a pair of cowboy boots in pink that had glass studs on them and enough bling to send her mother into a tirade for a week. She absolutely loved them.

"Oh, you have to get those." Rachel waved a hand at the pink boots. "They are so cute."

"They are, aren't they?" Gwyneth turned her foot

tapping her toe then her heel. They felt like fine leather gloves.

Rachel took a long sip of her red wine. "I love a good pair of cowboy boots. They're especially helpful when you need to kick a man to the curb."

"Uh, oh." Eve slipped out of a sleek pair of black Christian Louboutins. "That sounds rather strong for a general statement. Trouble in paradise?"

"Not anymore." Rachel shook her head.

Leah frowned. "Does this have something to do with Derek?"

Taking another sip of wine, Rachel shrugged. "I gave him the boot a couple of weeks ago."

"And you didn't tell your own sister?" Leah dropped her jaw. "Two years with this guy, one year of constant complaining, you finally decide to call it quits, and you wait till now to tell us?"

Rachel shrugged and stepped into a pair of high spike heels. "I was waiting until the sour taste wasn't in my mouth anymore."

"So this time you're really over?" Eve pushed the multitude of shoe boxes in front of her to one side and reached for a box of Manolo Blahnik shoes.

Nodding her head with enough force to snap off, Rachel sighed. "Haven't heard a word from him." She raised her wine glass. "I'm moving on."

Gwyneth did her best to keep track of why Rachel had broken off her relationship with Derek. Words like selfish, arrogant, clueless, and egotistical were flying around the room. No matter how hard she tried, Gwyneth simply couldn't keep up.

By the time she'd decided she absolutely wanted the pink boots, the women were laughing hilariously over a handful of jokes that had gone right over Gwyneth's head. They also agreed, with more wine in the handbag shop next door, that Rachel was much better off without that loser Derek. Gwyneth hoped they were right and that Rachel found someone new sooner than later. Everyone deserved to be as happy as Eve and Paige clearly were. Not that she dared to have dreams of happily ever after. Her mind drifted off to Mitch as a young man, and Mitch her knight in shining armor on the veranda, in her foyer, cutting down the tree, and in the barn. If she'd let herself, dreaming of happily ever after with Mitch at her side was simply too easy, but not very smart.

"Okay," Eve held a clutch purse in two hands, "this sucker is fantastic. It will match my new shoes perfectly."

Using what little money she had stashed in her private bank account from the sales of her boxes, Gwyneth bought the boots, but couldn't even begin to consider purchasing a purse to match.

"Oh, my." Leah jumped to her feet. "Look at the time. Grams is going to have a canary if we're much later."

"Agreed." Rachel slipped off the shoes she'd been trying on and reached for the two pairs she'd decided she couldn't live without. "Let's pay for our goodies and head back to the ranch."

As much fun as she'd had hanging out with the women in the Baron family, the entire day had been an exercise in killing time until she got to see Mitch again. It might not be smart to dream of a good-hearted and handsome man like Mitch falling for Plain Jane her, but she could certainly enjoy what little time together they had till the big date.

For days, all Mitch could think about was getting to DC, taking care of some business, and getting back as fast as he could. Not just because he didn't want to deal with Susan's increasing displays of personal interest, but because he really wanted to see Gwyneth again. The day spent chatting and truly getting to know the woman, not the first impressions, had been much more pleasant and even comfortable than he had expected. Biting his tongue and going through the motions in DC was becoming more and more challenging for him, all he wanted was to come home and be with the people he cared about. And nothing could have surprised him more than coming to grips with the understanding that he did fully and truly care about Gwyneth. Somehow they had to make sure that she got out from under Prudence's soul-crushing thumb. Today was just another stepping stone on the new path everyone was trying to help forge, and he could hardly wait to see how it went.

Seated in his favorite club chair in the family front parlor, he'd been scanning his grandfather's daily newspaper, pretending to actually care about what he was reading, when the front door opened and the sound of women's laughter rolled through the house. Immediately, a smile tugged at his lips. Setting the paper aside, he waited to see who was going to stroll into the room first.

Arms laden with shopping bags, Eve led the pack. Behind her, also carrying more than one bag each, Rachel then Leah came in, clearly still having a good time. He refrained from the urge to crane his neck or better yet, get up on his feet and see where was Gwyneth in all this? Just about to lose patience with his own battle of wills, the front door slammed shut and Paige and Gwyneth came laughing into the room. He had no idea what about an afternoon out shopping could be so entertaining, but obviously his family and friends knew. Friends. *Friend.* He liked that idea. He considered Gwyneth a friend now, and hoped she did the same.

"I see we had a productive day." His grandmother looked up from her favorite spot.

"More than productive." Eve pulled out a plain blue sleeveless dress in some kind of stretchy fabric. "I got this for a steal."

At the same moment, Paige spun around, holding a partially beaded black cocktail dress against her. "I have no idea where I'm going to wear this, but it kept calling to me, and who am I to not pay attention."

That made him chuckle softly. Where there was a good bargain to be had, his sisters would find a good reason to heed the call.

"What about you, dear?" Grams asked in Gwyneth's direction.

Her cheeks flushed the sweetest shade of pale pink.

"Go on," Eve nudged her, "show them."

Heaving in a deep breath, Gwyneth set the lone bag in her hand on the nearest chair and pulled out a large box. Removing the lid, she glanced up at the people in the room. "It's a bit much, but like everyone else, I couldn't resist." The brightest and shiniest pink cowboy boots he'd ever seen were now held out for all to see.

"Oh, they are adorable." Grams clapped her hands together. "I bet they're comfortable too."

"Like a pair of soft Italian gloves." Gwyneth nodded, the flicker of delight in her eyes momentarily dimmed before her gaze returned to the new purchase and a smile reappeared.

He'd have to find someplace to take her where she could wear the boots. Though he had a hard time imagining Prudence Van Klein letting her only daughter out the door in anything so colorful.

Hazel appeared in the doorway. "Supper is served."

"Oh, good." Eve dropped the dress back into the bag. "I am starving."

As the family moved into the dining room, Gwyneth returned her boots to the box and turning to follow the others, paused, her hand slowly reaching forward to something on the built-in bookcases that lined the wall.

Curious to see what had captured her attention, he inched closer, stopping beside her. "That's one of my grandmother's favorite pieces."

"It is?" Her fingers ran slowly over the small hand-carved box.

He nodded. "I saw it in the window of a small gift shop in the Heights. I knew Grams would love the detail and beautiful handwork. I bought one for her and one for Abbie." One side of his mouth tilted upward in just a hint of an amused smile. "I imagined some old sailor, bored with retirement, hunching over a plain wooden box and slowly turning it into a thing of beauty."

"Old sailor, huh?"

For the first time, following Gwyneth gently fingering

the box, he noticed that etched into the corner, completely camouflaged, was a set of initials. "I didn't realize the artist signed them."

"Artist," she uttered softly.

"Can you make them out?"

"G.V.K. It was easier than blending in G.J.V.K. Though newer boxes simply have G.V. engraved."

The way she almost reverently placed the box back on the shelf and then very slowly turned to face him before straightening her shoulder and holding a shaky smile, had his mind racing to connect the dots. Could it be?

"There aren't words to express how much it means to me that you like my work."

"You?"

She nodded.

"That's amazing." He reached around her and picked up the small box, seeing it with new eyes. The parallels didn't escape him. All the boxes had needed was for an artist to see their potential and bring it to life, and all Gwyneth needed was to see her own potential and let it shine through. Hopefully, all of his and his family's efforts would help her see her true value. "You're amazing."

Gwyneth blinked, but seemed to retreat to her silent persona.

"You should be very proud of these."

"Thank you." She glanced over at the box and back at him. "And yes, I'm very proud of my work, and cannot find the words to express how it feels knowing that both you and your grandmother like my boxes."

"More like love."

"Hey," Rachel stuck her head in the doorway, "you two planning on waiting for the daisies to bloom? We're famished, get the lead out." Just as quickly as she appeared, she disappeared down the hallway.

"I guess we'd better move to the dining room." He gestured after his cousin.

"Yes. Let's."

With everyone seated in the dining room and waiting for them, Grams pointed to the two, side by side, empty chairs. "Gwyneth, have a seat, dear."

Chatter filled the large room as each family member stood by the buffet, serving themselves, then retaking their seats. Mitch was still wrapping his mind around the boxes being made by Gwyneth. He couldn't help but wonder what other secrets and surprises did this woman have? She gave a whole new meaning to *peeling the onion.*

Halfway through the meal the conversation had gone from clothing, shopping, and fashion, to the ranch and new plans for the cattle and horses, to politics and Mitch's efforts with immigration.

"There has to be something we can do to make people see your way." Paige held her fork in midair.

"I'm trying, but it's hard to change people's preconceived notions." Mitch was slowly shifting from pushing as hard as he could to simply giving up.

Gwyneth set her fork on her plate and looked up, her mouth slightly open as if about to say something, then snapping it shut and retrieving her fork.

The way Paige and Eve sitting across from her continued to look in her direction, waiting, he figured they must have thought the same thing.

Finally, Eve set her fork down and leveled her gaze with Gwyneth. "Do you have any ideas?"

Gwyneth's gaze darted left, then right, then settled on Mitch.

"I'm open to all suggestions," he encouraged.

"Since the other day I've been thinking about it and something did occur to me."

"Really?" He shifted in his seat to better face her. "What?"

"You know the old cliché a picture is worth a thousand words?"

The people at the table nodded, but it was the Governor who spoke up. "Taking Congress to the border isn't helping anything."

She bobbed her head. "Agreed. There's plenty of media controlled coverage of the problems at the border. But what if some of your colleagues were to get a view not of the throngs huddled at the borders, but the ones already settled and struggling with day-to-day issues and fears?"

"Where are you going with this?" His mind was scrambling to keep up, but not succeeding.

"Texas is known for cowboys, barbecues, and everything being bigger and better."

Most everyone nodded.

"It's my understanding that if there's one thing politicians like, it's a good party. Especially one with lots of strong bankrolled guests."

Again, lots of heads nodded, someone muttered *sad but true*.

"What if you were to invite a handful of key colleagues who have been the hardest to convince. Bring them here on the Baron company jet—we don't want constituents accusing their representatives of flying to parties on the taxpayer's dime. Give them the good old Texas experience here on the ranch. A little cattle roping demonstration, maybe a barrel race or two, some good smoked barbecue."

Paige shook her head. "I don't see how that will help with new immigration legislation?"

"Ahh," Gwyneth raised her finger at the woman. "That's where the not so heavy bankrolled guests come in. Or more so, employees. We get the servers and other people who arrived as immigrants, illegal or not, and get casual conversations going with real people's stories and real people's fears."

"There are plenty of fears, that's for sure." Eve nodded, turning to her husband. "What was it that Marisol said the other day?"

"That the gang members crossing the border scare the folks already living and working here because they won't hesitate to steal and kill because they have no trackable footprints. The police have no way to associate them with the crimes they commit."

"Exactly." Gwyneth's face lit up. "Showing up at the border has a way of leaning toward photo ops and grandstanding. But at a family party, hearing these kinds of stories in casual conversation from people who have worked hard to build the American dream will go a lot farther to, shall we say, seeing the light. But there's a caveat."

"What's that?" the Governor asked.

"It would have to be thrown together quickly. If there's too much time, it could backfire into another photo op situation."

"Excellent point." The Governor sighed, then looked to Mitch. "What do you think?"

What he thought was that he loved the idea. Whether or not it would work was anyone's guess, but he was more than ready to do something outside of the box and was beyond flabbergasted that it had been Gwyneth who had come up with the idea. Then again, he was learning to expect the unexpected from this complex woman. "Brilliant. Just brilliant."

CHAPTER ELEVEN

"I am so excited, anyone would think I was the one coming out of a cocoon." Mitch's sister Eve stared at a plethora of gowns strewn across the bed.

"I hope Gwyneth isn't upset with us when she realizes we bought all the accessories that looked good on her when we were out shopping last week." Rachel's gaze shifted from the dresses to the shoes and other items on a dresser across the room.

"Well," Eve shrugged, "I'm sure she'll forgive us eventually."

Leah sighed. "I just hope she doesn't insist on wearing whatever it is her mother, or she, planned to wear."

"Have you seen it?" Rachel asked.

"No." Leah shook her head. "But based on her track record, we all know it wouldn't be good."

Only half listening to the conversation in the room, Mitch took in the fashion paraphernalia scattered about and wondered what the heck was going to happen here today. "What is all this?"

Rachel glanced left then right, one arm extended. "That's a hair dryer."

The only hair dryers he was familiar with were held in a hand. This sucker looked more like Rosie from the old *Jetsons'* cartoon.

"And that's a massage table."

Massage? Who needed a massage before dressing? He followed his cousin's finger as she pointed to one thing after another. "All the people to properly pamper and get everyone in shape will be here shortly. All we need now is our protégé."

Taking one more look around the room, he wondered if torture might not be a better word. "What time does this all start?"

Eve glanced down at her watch. "The manicurist should be here any minute. Who's picking up Gwyneth?"

"I am." Mitch raised his hand, though he wasn't so sure anymore that all this was a great idea.

"Good." Rachel walked up to him and pushed him out of the bedroom door. "You go. I'll let her know that you're on your way."

He blinked and shaking his head, said a quick prayer that when they were done torturing her, Gwyneth would still talk to him.

Gwyneth had barely gotten a lick of sleep last night. She was so excited and so bloody petrified. She'd played with different ways to style her unruly hair, each one looked more frightening than the next. At least, through the years, her hair had more of a wave than the ringlet mess it was as a child, but still, there was no way she wasn't going to be an embarrassment at Mitch's side.

Maybe she should just feign a stomachache or would throwing herself down the stairs and breaking a leg be too dramatic? Forcing one foot in front of the other, she looked at the gown hanging on her closet door. Lavender always made her look so washed out, and yet, that's the color her mother favored for her. At least she'd managed one little rebellion. She'd spent some of those waking hours last night ripping out the lace trim on the neckline and sleeves. The dress still was better suited to a woman from the turn of the last century, but at least it wasn't quite as obnoxious.

She had Mitch to thank for giving her just enough nerve to defy her mother. A little bit. Her mother would not be happy when she saw her in the dress, but by then it would be too late.

Taking a slow sip of water, she glanced at the clock on

the wall. Mitch had told her he'd be picking her up to dress with his sisters. Despite her explaining that her mother would never agree to it, he insisted it would be fine. She sure hoped he knew what he was talking about. For her mother, tonight was very important. Despite being Mitch's date for the evening, her mother had every intention of showing her off to Reginald Livingston. Prudence Van Klein was not going to let her out the door without first making sure that every strand of hair and layer of fabric was perfectly in place.

The sound of the doorbell pulled her out of her ruminations. This was it. The battle of wills was about to begin. The question at hand was did she have it in her to defy her mother outright if it came right down to it. Taking the dress carefully off the door, she picked up the overnight bag with her shoes and underthings and made her way downstairs, praying with every step that she wasn't about to walk into World War Three.

"There you are." Mitch's voice carried up from the bottom of the stairs.

Careful not to trip and tumble down the steps, she moved slowly.

Standing beside Mitch, her mother frowned up at her. "Child, child. You are not a housemaid. Put those things down." She waved at the butler. "Oliver, return those things to Gwyneth's room."

"Mother." She clutched the bag to her side and continued descending the steps.

"As for you, *Mister* Baron. My daughter is perfectly capable of dressing in her own home."

A tap sounded on the slightly open front door. "Excuse me. Though your car is very pretty, it's not very comfortable." Lila Baron eased her way into the foyer. "So good to see you again, Prudence. I understand our girls are going to be getting ready for tonight at my house. How fun to be young again, don't you think?"

"Well." Prudence stiffened and glanced up at her daughter coming off the last step.

"The gala is going to be the best yet. I am looking

forward to raising more money for charity than last year. Maybe the year before as well."

"Yes." Prudence was forced to tear her piercing gaze away from Gwyneth and smile for Lila. "I'm sure anything you're at the helm of will be an exemplary success."

Lila turned to Gwyneth. "I see you're all set. Good. We don't want to keep the girls waiting. I know you're going to have almost as much fun primping as you will dancing tonight." Without hesitating, she waved for Mitch to take Gwyneth's things, tucked Gwyneth's arm in hers and glancing over at her nemesis, grinned. "We'll see you tonight, Prudence."

Her mother had no choice but to smile and nod at Lila's departing back.

At the bottom of the steps, Mitch had already deposited her things in the trunk. With both car doors open and ready for her and his grandmother, he bowed at the waist and with a flourish waved one arm. "Your carriage awaits, fine ladies."

Still anxious about tonight, Mitch and Lila Baron's successful efforts to steal her from her own home had gone a long way to easing her nerves.

Settling into the back seat, Mitch leaned slightly inside and grinned at her. "Told you we had a plan."

For a long moment, he simply stood there and stared at her before stepping back and closing the door. The foolish young girl in her thought he might actually kiss her. The frumpy woman she was knew better.

In the driver's seat, Mitch tuned the ignition and pulled out of the driveway. "I put your things in the car, but we have a surprise for you at the house."

She was nervous enough about tonight, she wasn't sure she could handle anything more, but curiosity edged her nerves aside. "Really?"

"Really."

Lila spent the rest of the ride to the ranch filling her with stories of galas past. By the time they reached the house, Gwyneth's nerves were on full alert.

Standing in the foyer, she watched as Mitch brought in

her accessory bag and handed it to Oliver with instructions to take it upstairs. She waited another beat for him to retrieve her gown.

Instead of heading out the door, he opened a nearby closet and pulled out a long garment bag. "About that surprise."

"Yes."

"You have to promise to keep in mind that this gift comes with the best of intentions."

"Gift?"

He nodded and hooking the bag over the door, slowly unzipped it. Flashes of flowing red fabric caught her eye, and confusion set it. Another moment and the bag was fully unzipped and the beautiful dress that hung in the boutique window at the mall now hung from the Baron closet door.

"Eve gave me your size. If this doesn't fit, she has a backup for you, but I noticed how much you seemed to like it and I thought, well, I hoped—"

"It's beautiful," she cut him off.

He smiled. "Does this mean you're not upset with me?"

"I could never be upset with you." She fingered the fabric and wondered if she dared to wear anything so beautiful. "But I can't accept—"

This time he stopped her. "Please."

Overcome with emotion, the only thing she could manage was a nod. This man, who had been so special with her, had not only noticed that she was fascinated with this dress in the window, but remembered, and cared enough to buy it for her. Nodding slowly, she lifted her gaze to meet his. "Thank you."

"Thank *you*." He leaned in and gave her a quick peck on the cheek. "You'd better head upstairs before my sisters accuse me of kidnapping you."

"Yes, of course." She turned to reach for the dress.

"Oliver will bring it up."

"I can take it." Right now having something for her hands to do would be a good thing. "Really. It's fine."

He smiled and handed her the garment bag. Hurrying up the stairs, all she could think was how she was going to hate it when tonight drew to an end, and she returned to her miserable ivory tower.

In order to get ready for tonight, Mitch would need exactly thirty minutes. Forty, tops. One thing about living in Washington and finding himself invited to major events on a moment's notice was that he'd learned to dress quickly on the fly. Fifteen for a shower, and then the remainder to shave and put on his tux. Whether or not he needed the extra ten minutes was dependent upon whether the tie would cooperate.

"You look…unsettled." His grandmother lifted her gaze from her knitting.

"No. Just wondering why women need so much fuss for a single party."

"We don't need to, but it's fun. Almost like a bridal party."

That much was true. Both his sister Paige and Eve's wedding had meant a houseful of women primping and prepping, but he didn't remember this many people coming and going.

The parade had started a couple of hours ago. From the way the lone man to cross the threshold was dressed, Mitch was pretty sure he was the masseuse. After he'd left, two women came hurrying in each dragging a couple of small rolling suitcases behind them.

From there, the extra servers that had been setting up the grand ballroom at the rear of the house had been scurrying back and forth, occasionally taking trays of snacks and drinks. As the thoughts carried on in his mind, one of the aforementioned servers walked past the doorway heading to the stairs with another tray of orange and pink filled champagne flutes in hand.

"Are those mimosas or plain juice?" he asked.

Not lifting her head from her work, his grandmother didn't quite shrug. "Knowing Paige, I'd say the chances are excellent that those are mimosas or poinsettias."

If they kept serving drinks at this pace, the women were going to be three sheets to the wind before the actual party even started.

"How are we doing?" Craig and his wife, Kate, came through the doorway. Each one leaning over to kiss Grams hello. Kate carried a garment bag draped over her arm.

"Just fine." Grams looked to Kate. "Are you going to join the ladies?"

Kate smiled. "Yes. I hope I'm in time to catch the stylist."

"No massage?" Mitch teased.

Kate frowned. "Massage?"

"Never mind." Mitch waved her off. "But you might want to hurry before the last batch of mimosas are gone."

"Ooh. I love mimosas." She raised up on her tippy toes and kissed her husband lightly on the lips. "Don't leave your tux in the car too long or it will get all wrinkled."

Craig pulled her back for another quick kiss and then patted her rear as she hurried away, his gaze lingering on her back until she disappeared across the hall and up the stairs.

Normally, seeing his brothers watch their wives with so much love in their eyes always pricked at Mitch's heart. He understood that with time, the ache inside would ease, but not feeling that familiar pang of regret now caught him by surprise. Twirling the ring on this left hand, he twisted it off and let the weight of it sit in his palm a long moment before slipping it back on. Was that how it happened? One day the ache was as real and strong as the day before, and then, just like that, it was gone?

"Okay." Craig clasped his hands together. "It's past my lunch time and I'm starved."

So intent on watching the comings and goings up and down the stairs, Mitch had lost all track of time. And hunger. "I could stand to eat."

"I'll see what Hazel has fixed. Things have been pretty busy." His grandmother set her knitting aside, and the two fur balls at her feet began swishing their tails like a metronome. "You two stay here. It's human lunch time."

"You don't need to get up." Craig waved her down. "I can check."

"I'll go with you." Mitch stood. He might as well eat with his brother. From what he could see, it was going to be a long day.

The sound of footsteps on the stairs met him as he stepped into the foyer. To his surprise, wrapped in a white terrycloth robe with a matching towel around her head, Gwyneth almost plowed into him.

"Oh, excuse me." Clutching at the top of her robe with one hand and the towel on her head with the other, she took a step in retreat. "The phone in Eve's room isn't working. She wants Hazel to bring up some of her special low-cal quesadillas."

His gaze raked over her. The robe barely covered her knees. This was the first time he'd seen her in anything that showed that much leg. And to his surprise, what little he could see was quite shapely.

Craig cleared his throat and Mitch's head shot up, his gaze leveling with hers. "We were just on our way to the kitchen. I can tell Hazel if you'd like?"

Her cheeks flushed a pale pink, she slowly nodded her head. "Thank you. I'd appreciate that." Without waiting, she spun around and hurried up the stairs.

"Careful, big brother." Craig sighed and headed for the kitchen.

Mitch stared after the empty stairwell. A very long day, and something told him, an even longer night.

CHAPTER TWELVE

As expected from Lila Baron, Paradise Ridge had been transformed into a holiday wonderland. White lights reminiscent of twinkling fairies draped the outdoors. Trees sparkled, shrubs twinkled, and oohs and aahs would no doubt fill the air upon guests' arrivals. Inside, decked with poinsettias and standing candelabras, the home warmly invited the attendees to follow the path to the rear of the house, teasingly dubbed "the ballroom" by the family.

When Lila wasn't throwing a gala or fundraiser for some organization or other, the huge indoor space functioned as a family entertainment venue. Pool table, ping pong, air hockey, pinball, anything that a teenager, or adult still a teen at heart, would love. A portion of the room could be quickly draped off for theater style viewing on a large screen. But tonight, all the furnishings and toys had been moved to one of the barns, and the space resembled the brilliance of a royal ball. Tables dispersed around the perimeter of the dance floor were arranged to allow for friendly conversation from table to table. The low centerpieces of crystal and candles added to the sensation of a winter wonderland.

"She's done it again." Cooper stood by his cousin taking in the surreal dream world their grandmother had created.

Smiling at the winter wonderland around them, Mitch nodded. "Every year her themes astound me."

"I rather liked last year." CJ, Chase's wife, stopped at their side. "Something about cowboy hats and boots with a tux or evening gown was simply fascinating."

Only his grandmother could blend black-tie elegance with cowboy casual. It had been a money-making hit for the organization. "It was quite fun." And in his favorite boots, his feet didn't hurt at the end of the night.

Looking over her shoulder, CJ focused on the three sets of double French doors. "Where are Paige and Eve?"

"Good question." How long did those women need to get ready anyhow? Wasn't all day enough?

"I can hear the chatter in the foyer." Craig came up behind them, quickly surveying the room. "The show is about to begin. Places, everybody."

"Oh, for the love of Henry." CJ rolled her eyes. "Once a movie producer, always a movie producer."

"Who's Henry?" Cooper's brows buckled in confusion.

CJ shrugged. "No clue, but my English grandmother always said that. I guess it stuck."

The text alert on Mitch's wristwatch buzzed and he glanced down. "It's Eve. She wants me by the stairs."

"What for?" Craig asked.

"They're ready." He turned toward the door.

CJ, a former Marine and the least likely to spend a day primping of all his female relatives, twisted one side of her face. "They need an audience?"

"I suspect," Craig moved to follow his brother, "more of a grand entrance."

Cooper snapped his fingers. "That's right. Rachel was telling me that they're going all Cinderella on Gwyneth."

It only took a few steps for him to realize he had an entourage following him. He wasn't sure if that was what his sister wanted, but he wasn't going to stop them. At the foyer, a trickle of guests had already arrived, chatting with his grandmother and the Governor, slowly making their way through the entry to the ballroom, pausing every few steps to greet another person.

Near the bottom of the stairs, he found himself cornered by one guest and then another, each one either praising him for a job well done, or fussing about something they felt he should be doing. Anxious to reach the steps as his sister had requested, the sound of giggling and coaxing floated down from the second-floor landing. Within seconds, a collective gasp reached his ears. Noticing the stunned look on his family's faces, he glanced up. The figure of a woman in a deep red dress stood poised at the top of the steps, a tentative smile graced her delicate features. Understanding dawned and he almost swallowed his tongue. Good heavens. Gwyneth.

Mitch had no idea what he'd expected, but nothing had prepared him for this moment. Chestnut-brown hair, glistening under the light, framed her face. A very nervous face. The shimmering red dress hugged every curve and flared loosely from her hips giving the appearance of a goddess.

"Wow," a voice behind him exclaimed. "Who's that?"

"Gwyneth Van Klein," he muttered.

"That can't be… Holy Christmas, it is."

He had no idea who had said what, but the murmurings behind him continued and he had an unexpected urge to scream to them all that she was his. And where the heck had that come from?

Taking short, deep breaths, Gwyneth prayed she wouldn't collapse in a panic attack, or worse, take a nose dive down the staircase.

"You've got this," Eve murmured behind her.

She pasted on a smile and reached for the railing, but her feet didn't seem to want to move. All day she'd felt like an old rag in a Chinese laundry. Plucked, snipped, scrubbed, polished, and shoved into a skin-tight gown, she felt stiffer than a starched shirt. When the hairdresser first announced that the yards of hair pinned to the back of her head needed to go, she almost passed out from lack of oxygen, until she realized the woman was absolutely right. What did it matter that her mother didn't believe in short hair? Looking at the woman with scissors in hand, Gwyneth smiled. "Cut it."

Once she'd gotten over that moment of near terror, she

found nearly every inch of her had been waxed and slathered in oils and creams until she was slicker than an eel. Her feet scrubbed and scraped and her nails polished a deep shade of Christmas red, the only thing she could think of was how much her mother disapproved of polish. After all, ladies didn't chew gum, whistle, or wear red anything. Yet, here she was practically draped in all things red.

The true shock had come not with the loss of hair or the bright fingernails shining up at her every time she moved her hand. No, the true shock had come when her facial had been complete and her makeup applied. Sitting up to see herself for the first time, her mouth fell open at how big and bright her blue eyes looked without a caterpillar of bushy eyebrows to shadow them. Had that really been her reflection in the mirror? She looked… normal. For the first time since agreeing to be Mitch's date, she actually felt she might not be an embarrassment to him. That is, as long as she made it down the stairs one foot at a time and not head over heels.

Sucking in a deep breath, she searched the growing crowd below for a familiar face. Almost instantly she homed in on Mitch. Eyes wide with the same shock she'd felt at her first glimpse of herself, a sweet lazy smile slowly stretched across his face. He was pleased. That simple show of approval gave her legs the ability to move forward. One foot at a time, she slowly descended the grand staircase. Holding her head up high had come easily. No need to hide in a corner, or avert her gaze.

The last two steps were the easiest. Mitch had moved closer to the staircase and waited with an extended hand. "Hello."

"Hello," she softly spoke.

"You're radiant." His grip held her hand tightly as she stepped onto the hardwood floor. "Absolutely radiant."

No one else bustling about the foyer en route to the main party seemed to care about her or her entrance. Even the other Barons standing at his side had given her a quick nod followed by a simple, *you look lovely* before following the flow of people to the back of the house.

The best part of all, for every step from the staircase to the grand ballroom, Mitch held onto her hand, the warmth of his touch infusing her with a strength she didn't know she had. Suddenly, she no longer cared about her mother's lengthy list of dos and don'ts. All she cared about was the man at her side. No sooner had they crossed into the massive room, then the orchestra began to play.

"Shall we?" Mitch's smile seemed fragile, as if he thought there was any way in hell she was going to say no.

"I would love to."

At first, she'd feared the nearly strapless dress with lacey thin arm sleeves that stretched across from the neckline and not from the shoulders would restrict her ability to move her arms. Quickly, Eve had pointed out that the fashion statement would accentuate her porcelain shoulders without issue. Her hand in Mitch's and the other holding the loop at the hem of her skirt to keep her from tripping, her ease of movement had proved Eve correct.

As they spun around the floor to the magical tunes of eras long gone, Gwyneth could feel eyes on her and hear the soft murmurings as she and Mitch swept past them. The difference, of course, this time there were no snickers or laughs. Nothing to tease her for. Though she was pretty sure not a one realized who she was. She wasn't all too sure she recognized herself either. A few people dancing past them would slow and smile at their US Senator, others would take a moment to say hello or offer some other positive comment about his representation, but the soft gasps of the few who had put two and two together and come up with Gwyneth Van Klein, actually made her smile.

"You've made quite an impression on people." Mitch spun her around.

"You've improved."

His eyebrow lifted.

"Your dancing. Since my presentation to society."

He dipped his chin. "I'd like to think I'm better at a lot of things since those days."

She just knew her cheeks were flaming rosy red at the possibilities that had popped into her mind.

"Gwyneth, dear, is that you?" Ida Bloom, one of her mother's bridge partners, almost tripped her husband when she stopped short on the dance floor. "Astonishing, just astonishing."

"Yes." She smiled at the old busy body. "Mrs. Baron is so gifted at these wonderful parties."

Ida blinked, her eyes narrowing and then in a flash, her plastic smile returned. "Why yes, yes of course. Delightful wonderland."

Before the woman could say another word, Mitch spun them around and danced her out of Ida's earshot. "You're sure you've never been in politics? That was a masterful redirect. Had to bite my tongue not to laugh at how easily you put her in her place."

"I'm sure she won't be the last once word gets out."

As if she'd shot off a starter gun, the rest of the dance was spent evading and politely responding to a slew of women, all stunned at her transformation. Not that she could blame them, she herself had been beyond stunned when she finally saw herself in the mirror. The way her dress exposed a tantalizing hint of cleavage and bare shoulder, then tightly wrapped around her waist, the flow of shimmering fabric draping over her hips and falling loosely to the floor. Swishing with every step, the gown gave her an hourglass figure that easily masked what Rachel had called comfortably padded hips. Expanding that no real man liked skin and bones. She had to wonder if Mitch was among the men who would appreciate *comfortably padded hips*. Then again, after tonight, she had no business imagining anything. For now, her only job was to enjoy what little time she had until the stroke of midnight when Cinderella turned back into a wallflower.

All she wanted to do was enjoy the magic of the night, and dancing in Mitch's arms.

The melodic golden oldie made popular by Fred Astaire came to a stop and to her chagrin, Mitch stepped out of her personal space. "Shall we sit this one out?"

She nodded. Her shoes were surprisingly comfortable, but a break would be good. And something to drink. "I am a bit thirsty."

"Let's have a seat and I'll get you a refreshment. Champagne?"

Oh, how she loved champagne. "That would be lovely, thank you."

Mitch remained standing behind her as she seated herself at the family table.

"Gwyneth Justine," her full Christian name came out of her mother's mouth like a tightly spoken curse word. *And let the fireworks begin.*

CHAPTER THIRTEEN

"**M**other." Gwyneth had been bracing herself all day for Prudence Van Klein's reaction, now she had to remind herself not to crumble at the woman's harsh tone.

"Mrs. Van Klein. How nice to see you again." Mitch took a step closer to Gwyneth's mother, literally placing himself between Gwyneth and the impending onslaught. "Could I interest you in something to drink?"

"Thank you, but I have all I need at my table."

"Very well." He rested his hands on Gwyneth's shoulder, unbeknownst to him, imparting his strength as he leaned over and whispered in her ear, "I won't be long. You can do this."

Could she? She came within inches of grabbing his hand and begging him not to leave. But he was right. What had to be said next needed to be between her mother and herself and no one else. She'd have preferred an alternate time or place, but obviously her mother thought differently.

"Won't you have a seat, Mother?" She waved at Mitch's empty chair beside her.

"I have my own seat." Prudence seemed to be grinding her teeth as she formed the next words she wanted to share. "I can't even begin."

"Then perhaps you shouldn't." Gwyneth stood. "Oh, Mother. I don't want to quarrel. Can't we enjoy this lovely evening and put petty differences aside?"

For a long moment, Gwyneth saw fire in her mother's eyes. "Petty?"

"Mother. You know what I mean."

"Do I?" Prudence Van Klein did what she'd done so

well for as long as Gwyneth could remember. Lifting her chin and throwing already erect shoulders back, she straightened to her full height, glared at Gwyneth, and teeth still grinding, softly enunciated, "You are not my daughter."

Before Gwyneth could process the words thrown in her direction, her mother had turned and marched away. Not to her seat, but straight ahead and through the double doorways. Was her mother leaving? Did she really mean what she'd said? Could a woman discard her own flesh and blood that easily? Could it be that overnight Gwyneth would go from being a member of one of the wealthiest families in the State of Texas to a homeless beggar?

"Perhaps you should go after her." Lila Baron had quietly come up beside her. "She's upset. Most likely gone to the ladies' room to avoid creating a scene."

Heaven forbid her mother created a scene. Real emotions and public displays of affection were high on her mother's do not do list for proper young ladies.

"Be patient. This is a lot of change for her too. She'll need time to adjust."

Gwyneth nodded at one of the kindest, most caring women she'd ever known. "Thank you. Please tell Mitch where I am."

"Of course, dear."

Drawing from the earlier strength she'd felt, in complete contrast to the terrifying turmoil churning inside her, she casually strolled out of the ballroom toward the bathroom designated for ladies. Slowly, her finger wrapped around the doorknob, and drawing in a very long deep breath, she exhaled as she turned the knob and pushed the door open.

As expected, her mother stood at the sink, staring into the mirror. Her white knuckled grip threatening to rip the pedestal sink from the floor.

"Mother."

Rather than turn to face her only daughter, Prudence Van Klein followed Gwyneth's movement in the mirror. "What have you to say for yourself? You should be ashamed."

Doing as her mother had taught her, she stood perfectly straight, and perfectly still. "I have nothing to be ashamed of, and neither do you."

"How dare you tell me what I should and should not be ashamed of. When I think of all the years and care I've bestowed on you. My recompense for a child of my old age should have been a comfort in my senior years. I find no comfort in your deliberate disregard for all that is decent and—"

"There is nothing indecent about any of this. As for your intentions for my life, things cannot go back to the way they were. I am a woman fully grown. I expect to be given the independence and respect commensurate with my age and standing in the community."

"Standing in the community? Look at you. Look at your hair," the angry woman almost spat her words. "A woman's hair should be her pride and joy." Her one arm shot up in Gwyneth's direction. "And colored, no less."

"Highlights. They look quite natural. Everyone has been very complimentary about my new hairstyle."

"Again you place more value on the opinions of heathens than the teaching of your own mother. You might not be so full of yourself if I no longer offered you the refuge of my home, providing for all your needs. Maybe that would change your tune."

"I'm not afraid of your threats, Mother." *Not afraid.* She wasn't afraid. "I imagine I could get a job, earn my own way. Live my own life."

"And does living your own life mean behaving like nothing more than a trollop, a street urchin, a—"

"That's enough, Mother. This tyrannically dysfunctional imitation of mothering has to stop."

Once more her mother's eyes lit with fury and the muscles in her jaw twitched with anger. "How dare you—"

"Mother, please." Closing her eyes, Gwyneth turned her back, gathering her wits, her courage, and then, taking in a deep breath, spun back around. "Perhaps I was a bit harsh. If only we could find some middle…gr..ou…nd…. Mother?"

Staring icily at the mirror, her mother failed to move, to blink, to breathe. Her viselike grip on the sink eased as her mouth twisted to one side of her face and her eyes slowly rolled back in her head.

"Mother!" Gwyneth leapt forward in an effort to reach her mother before her limp body fell to the floor and a panicked cry tore from her throat, "Help!"

Having left the two glasses of champagne on the table, Mitch was on his way to wait for Gwyneth outside the ladies room. His grandmother had told him what she'd overheard Prudence say to her daughter. He could not imagine anything more painful for someone as sensitive as Gwyneth. So much of who she was deep down had begun to emerge, showing a strong, talented, smart, and capable woman. Someone who listened patiently, spoke eloquently, and offered unwavering support. The thought of her retreating into her shell, slipping away from him, and back into the clutches of that woman made his heart physically ache.

With every step he took, fury simmered in his blood. Never in his life had he wanted to outright slug a woman before. Though that would be too simple a punishment for Prudence. Gwyneth deserved so much more from a mother. He'd made it just outside the door when Gwyneth's blood-curdling scream for help blasted into the hall. Ladies room or no ladies room, he bolted inside the small bathroom.

Unconscious, Prudence Van Klein lied motionless in Gwyneth's arms.

Her eyes closed, Gwyneth softly repeated, "It's my fault, my fault."

"Gwyneth." He collapsed to his knees beside her. "What happened?"

"I did it." Were the only words to escape her lips as she rocked with her mother.

Craig's head popped in the doorway. "What's wrong?"

"I don't know. Call an ambulance and someone find CJ." He turned back to Gwyneth, feeling woefully unprepared, he had no idea what to do for her. "Help is coming."

"My fault, all my fault."

"Shh. It's all right. Everything will be fine. You'll be fine."

CJ came bursting through the door and rushed to Prudence's side. Didn't they all make an odd scene. Three women in evening gowns, on the floor. "What happened?"

"I have no idea." Mitch shook his head, completely lost.

"Gwyneth." CJ put her hand on Gwyneth's forearm. "I need you to tell me what happened."

Gwyneth did not say a single word. Not even her recent mantra of *it's my fault*.

"Did she fall?" CJ asked, checking the prone woman's pulse.

Silence from Prudence's daughter.

Shaking her arm, CJ nearly shouted, "Gwyneth. I need to know what happened. Did she fall? Hit her head?"

Gwyneth blinked, then shook her head.

"Did she say anything before she fell unconscious?" CJ tried again.

"It's my fault," Gwyneth mumbled.

"Gwyneth! Snap out of it." CJ was in full Marine command voice. "Did she clutch her chest? Have slurred speech? Tell me!"

Chase's head popped in this time. "Ambulance will be here any minute." His gaze flew to CJ. He didn't need to say a word, even Mitch could see the worry in his brother's eyes.

"Her pulse is steady. I can't tell if it's a stroke, a seizure, an allergic reaction. I have nothing to go on." CJ returned her attention to Prudence, checking for evidence of a head wound.

Every second passed as if taking hours. Mitch had never been so relieved as he was at the words someone shouted through the now propped open doorway. "EMTs are here."

Another moment and two burly men along with a half a dozen firemen were crammed into the tight restroom. Mitch had practically needed a crow bar to pry Gwyneth away from her mother. Maneuvering her out of the way, he stood to one side with his family as the EMTs put Prudence on oxygen, on the gurney, and then hurried out the door with her.

To his surprise, the party was still in full force in the other room. His siblings had jumped into action, keeping the area clear of wandering guests. Redirecting people to the other bathrooms on the floor. Making sure the EMTs had a clear path to Prudence. As far as most of the guests knew, this portion of the house had been closed off for a minor spill in need of cleaning up. None of them may have served in the military, but their Marine grandfather had taught them all well.

Cradling Gwyneth to his side, he ushered her out the front door and into his car. "We're following the ambulance to the hospital."

"My fault," she mumbled, only this time, she seemed more grounded in reality and no longer in her own head. "We quarreled. I called her petty, tyrannical, dysfunctional."

He refrained from telling her that she'd pretty much nailed the description of her mother's behavior. "Shh." He reached over and squeezed her hand. "None of this is your fault. Your mother is no spring chicken."

"I should have been more sensitive. More aware. She's old. Fragile."

"Fragile? Honey, please. Don't torture yourself. These things happen. Whatever has struck your mother would most likely have happened if you quarreled with her or if someone at her table used the wrong fork. Face it. Your mother is older and a bit high strung." That was the nicest thing he could say about Prudence Van Klein.

"I still should have known better. This is all my fault."

Turning the corner into the hospital's emergency room parking lot, he said a silent prayer. Getting Gwyneth through the next few hours without having a nervous breakdown was going to take more wisdom than he possessed. But he'd already lost one woman he cared about, he couldn't let anything happen to Gwyneth too.

CHAPTER FOURTEEN

Having shucked his tuxedo jacket, tie, and cummerbund hours ago, Mitch rubbed his eyes and made his way to the family dining room in a desperate search for strong coffee. He'd refused to leave Gwyneth's side all night, convinced without someone watching over her, she might wind up in a bed beside her mother. He was terrified of what today might bring.

"Is she asleep?" His grandmother looked up from her seat at one end of the massive table.

"The meds the doc gave her finally kicked in."

"It was smart of you to bring her here. No sense in being cooped up alone in that mausoleum of a home." His grandmother had most likely been up all night the same as half his family. Convincing Gwyneth to stay at the ranch had been no easy task. Each member of his family had done many things in his lifetime to make him proud to be a Baron, but nothing as much as the way they had rallied around Gwyneth, all wanting to do whatever they could for her at a difficult time that could very well only get worse.

Chase and CJ had gone with them to the hospital. Having a sister-in-law with a medical background had come in quite handy as they maneuvered the system. Somewhere at the crack of dawn the doctors had come out to speak to a still numb Gwyneth. The final conclusion: a massive stroke. It had taken him and CJ close to an hour to convince Gwyneth that her mother would not be waking up anytime soon and that Gwyneth needed to get some rest.

The rest part was the challenge. Overwrought and taking the blame for her mother's condition, getting Gwyneth to stop beating herself up had been more difficult than dealing with Congress. It was CJ who convinced her that a mild sedative would allow her to get much-needed sleep. Not till Mitch promised to wake her up if anything changed did she finally acquiesce.

"I spoke with her brother Rupert again this morning." Chase had been the one to reach out to Gwyneth's three brothers. One was on a business trip in Chicago and expected home some time today, another was vacationing out of the country, but Rupert and his wife had abandoned theater plans and rushed to the hospital.

"Anything we didn't know last night?"

Chase nodded. "Quite a bit."

Something in his tone had Mitch stopping mid pour.

"For starters, he spoke with the family physician. Apparently, Prudence has been having issues with mini-strokes and didn't tell anyone in the family. Her doctor also told her that if she didn't get her blood pressure under control, something like this might happen."

"She probably thought she was invincible." His grandmother shook her head slowly in silent disapproval.

"There's more. It seems that Rupert got the family attorney out of bed at an indecent hour this morning."

"Hmm," Mitch muttered. Already the vultures were circling.

"To his and his brothers' surprise," Chase continued, "as the eldest, he is not the one given power of attorney."

Returning to pouring his coffee, the news didn't surprise him. Rupert was as arrogant as his mother, but Calvin the middle brother was the one who truly ran Klein Electronics. "Which brother has it?"

"Not brother. Sister. Gwyneth has the full general power of attorney as well as medical power of attorney. And for what it's worth, Prudence Van Klein is not only still the majority stock holder of Klein electronics and a dozen other companies, she's the deciding vote on a handful of board of directors that even I had no idea she was involved with."

"Well, I'll be." His grandmother looked to her husband. "I wouldn't be surprised if Prudence's sudden interest in marrying her daughter off didn't have something to do with her own sense of mortality."

"Maybe." The Governor merely shook his head. "Whatever the reason, I certainly hope Gwyneth is up to stepping into her mother's shoes."

At this moment, Mitch wasn't sure Gwyneth was up to brushing her teeth, never mind taking over for her mother. If he thought he didn't understand Prudence Van Klein before, he certainly didn't understand her now. Coffee cup in hand, his gaze rose to the ceiling as if he could see through to the guest room where Gwyneth slept. Now what the heck was going to happen?

Vile words like petty, tyrannical, dysfunctional and imitation of mothering replayed in Gwyneth's head over and over. Her own voice torturing her. The frightened look in her mother's eyes. The monstrous contortion of her face moments before collapsing on the cold, hard bathroom floor. Gwyneth sprang up, shaking her head.

Slowly scrubbing at her face in a vain effort to wash her mind, she opened her eyes. Blinking, she focused on a mirror ahead. The reflection staring back at her looked much less orderly than last night, but the pieces were falling into place. She'd been brought out of the image of twentieth century spinsterhood into the new millennium. And almost killed her mother in the process.

Literally squeezing her face, hoping to shove every painful memory far away, she sucked in a breath and looked away from the mirror. Left then right, she took in the classic yet modern décor of a room she did not recognize. Where was she? Shoving the painful memories of her mother's collapse and rush to the hospital, the gravely voice of the physician informing her that Prudence Van Klein had suffered a massive stroke, she forced herself to focus on where she was and why she was here.

Snapshots of Mitch at her side in the house, helping her

into the car, arranging for her and his family to wait in a private lounge for news. Then she remembered the warmth of his touch as his arm draped around her, holding her close, murmuring reassuring words. That particular vision was almost enough to bring a smile to her lips. Almost. She had no right to be happy at Mitch's attention while her mother had suffered so painfully.

More recollections of the passing hours came flooding back. Chase's wife CJ going toe to toe with the medical staff, pulling information they didn't want to share, demanding attention they were slow to give. Chase reaching out to her brothers, and then upon Rupert's arrival, dealing with him as if they had been lifelong chums and not new acquaintances. All of which brought her to the here and now. Still foggy in her mind, she remembered Mitch insisting she didn't need to be alone and bringing her back to the ranch. He and CJ insisting she needed to rest and giving her something the doctor prescribed, then bringing her up to this room to sleep.

Had she slept? Turning to the night side table, she spotted an antique grandmother clock. Good grief. It was past eleven. Looking down at herself, she was no longer in her evening gown, but who… right… Eve and CJ had helped her change into a nightgown, but now what? She couldn't very well go downstairs in pajamas. Maybe she could find a robe in the closet. Her mother would never approve of descending the stairs without being properly dressed, but then again, her mother was in no condition to dictate propriety to her. Stepping into a pair of slippers at the foot of the bed, she noticed fresh clothing draped across the back of a chair. Walking over, she quickly looked over the outfit. A short sleeve sheath dress, much like what she'd admired Eve in the day of the tea. In her size, the dress looked new. Did the Barons keep spare wardrobe available for unexpected guests or had Mitch arranged to purchase more clothes for her along with last night's gown?

Either way, it didn't matter now. Gathering the dress and underthings in her arm, she sought out the adjoining bathroom. A shower and clean clothes would do wonders to wake her up. Coffee would be nice too. Just then her stomach growled, reminding her she had not yet eaten last night. Perhaps coffee and toast. So, her mother wouldn't be staring daggers at her after all. She would descend the stairs more than properly dressed. The new Gwyneth Van Klein was about to make her first entrance into her new world. Or maybe she was only fooling herself, living one more day in the dream that had been before the nightmare.

"Should someone go check on her?" At the table for lunch, Mitch looked to his grandmother.

"I already looked in before I came down." Rachel, who along with his sisters and CJ, had decided to stay at the ranch in case she could be of help, smiled at him. "She was snug as a bug in a rug."

Maybe he should have listened to his grandmother and gotten a couple hours of shut eye. On his hundredth cup of coffee and second wind, he'd been afraid if he fell asleep, he'd not be able to wake up when Gwyneth did. At least he'd taken the time to shower, shave, and put on some comfortable clothes. Fully dressed, standing by his night table, the ring on his left hand caught a glint of light. Frozen in place, if asked in a court of law, he might have been willing to swear he heard Abbie softly ask him, *don't you think it's time*? Sliding the ring off his finger and securing it in the top drawer had been easier than he'd expected. He wondered how long it would take for the tan line to disappear and waited for something akin to remorse or regret to overtake him and have him shoving the ring back on his finger. Another moment and he'd walked away from the nightstand and the ring and made his way downstairs.

"Good morning," Gwyneth's soft-spoken voice snapped him away from his thoughts and had him jumping out of his seat.

Hurrying to meet Gwyneth at the doorway, he barely touched her arm. "How are you feeling?"

Blinking and forcing a weak smile, she leveled her gaze with his. "I've had better days, but under the circumstance, fine. And hungry."

"Good." He settled one hand at the base of her back and steered her toward the side buffet laden with today's lunch choices. "Hazel has been cooking all morning. I think she was expecting an army for lunch."

"Bless Hazel," was all Gwyneth said as she picked up the ladle and served herself a bowl of red soup.

Grams' eyes followed her every move. "Hazel thought some tomato bisque would be soothing."

"Lots of antioxidants in tomatoes," Rachel added, taking in the multiple glares that had suddenly swung in her direction. "Well, there are."

To his surprise, the little family interaction brought a very slight smile to Gwyneth's face as she took a seat. "Tomatoes are very healthy. Thank you, everyone."

"I've been keeping tabs with the hospital," the Governor addressed Gwyneth. "Your mother is still resting comfortably. Several tests have been scheduled to determine the extent of the damage."

"I should go." Gwyneth rose from her seat.

"Not till you've eaten." His Grams waved her back down. "You need your strength too."

"Yes, ma'am." Gwyneth lowered herself into the chair again and took her first sip of soup.

The Governor looked to Mitch and raised his brows at him. Mitch knew what he was asking. Should they tell her now about her newfound power or wait? He honestly didn't know what to do. Calling his relationship with Gwyneth atypical was an understatement. He wasn't even sure if relationship was the right word, though he certainly hoped she would agree that they were now indeed friends. And friends don't keep secrets. So ready or not, surrounded by people who truly cared about her—after all, her own brother had not offered his home to her when they'd left the hospital—now was as good a time as any to update her on her new responsibilities. "Chase spoke with Rupert earlier today."

Her gaze lifted to meet his. "News on Mother?"

"Not medical news. No." He shook his head, then reached over to take hold of her free hand. "Gwyneth, you have your mother's medical and general power of attorney."

The soup spoon dropped with a clank against the nearly empty bowl. "Me?"

He nodded.

"Why me?" She frowned, looking from him to the others at the table.

"I wish I had answers for you. Even your brothers were surprised at the information."

Gwyneth nodded. "She commented recently that when she passed I would be the most powerful Van Klein in the family. I thought she was mocking me."

"Apparently not," the Governor said.

Shaking her head, she stared at the bowl in front of her. Mitch could feel her hand begin to tremble, so he squeezed it hard, delighted when she turned to face him.

"You got this." Those were the same words he'd said last night. He'd meant them then and meant them now. Day by day he'd come to learn that an amazing woman of great knowledge and instinct was buried under the frumpy façade. "Which brings another thing to mind."

Her gaze narrowed.

"You're going to have your hands full for a while, at least until things settle with your mother. Since it was your idea, I really wanted to have you here for the Texas barbecue in two weeks."

She bobbed her head and actually almost smiled.

"As I said, you're going to have your hands full so I've left word with my staff to postpone. Maybe in the spring."

"That will be too late." She frowned at him. "We agreed that speed was of the essence. The element of almost surprise is in your favor. The more time everyone has to think about it and scheme, the lower the chances of success. You can't postpone."

"I don't want to host this without you here. This is your baby as much as mine. It has to wait."

"I can do it." The way her shoulders straightened and

her chin lifted, he could see every drop of Van Klein breeding making an appearance. More importantly, he saw a confidence in her eyes that he didn't think he'd see after last night's fiasco.

"Are you sure?" He had to ask even though he knew the answer.

"I'm positive. I'll deal with whatever Mother needs, and I'll be here for the rootinest tootinest Texas-style barbecue your colleagues have ever seen."

"That's my girl." He just prayed that the mantle of responsibility laid on her shoulders wouldn't be enough to weigh her down or break her spirit. For now he had every intention of having her back every step of the way—if she'll let him.

CHAPTER FIFTEEN

How had two weeks flown by so quickly? Gwyneth's head was spinning with all the people who needed something from her. She knew full well that her mother attended miscellaneous board meetings and took calls from division heads of Klein Electronics and its subsidiaries, but she assumed Prudence was merely looking over her brothers' shoulders. She didn't have a clue that her mother actually had the final word on just about everything.

At first, her inclination was to merely allow her brothers and the boards to continue business as usual, giving them the final word on all matters. Mitch, however, had convinced her that her mother was many things—stupid was not one of them. If she'd chosen Gwyneth, then she shouldn't hand the power over to her brothers.

Unexpected inflammation had the doctors keeping her mother in an induced coma. So Gwyneth spent the first week of her waking hours in her mother's room reading all the quarterly reports for the last two years as well as everything on paper she could get her hands on. The reading had made the silence of the room easier to bear. It had also selfishly stopped her from replaying that night in the bathroom over and over in her mind.

Mitch had helped more than he could possibly know. Suggesting she stay at the ranch that first week, listening carefully when she asked questions regarding some of the things she noticed in the reports, and receiving what she'd deemed wise and respectful council.

Thinking back to that first night she'd dared to speak up brought a smile to her face. The math simply wasn't adding up when she compared the stock holder reports to the in-office memos. She could see actual pride in Mitch's face when he informed her that the problem was not with her interpretation, but with the reporting, and encouraged her to dig deeper. Had she ever seen pride in anyone's eyes when looking at her? No, she was sure that look was a first for her.

On top of having a man who seemed genuinely interested in her thoughts and ideas, staying at the ranch with all the comings and goings of the vast family members had allowed her to get closer to the women her age. It was nice having friends. Very nice. Besides the perk of being near to Mitch, staying at the ranch had also allowed her to be more involved in the preparations for the big barbecue, at least when she wasn't inundated with reports.

By the time her mother came out of the coma, her deficiencies were obvious, and her stubbornness even more evident. Despite the difficulties in speaking due to the complete paralysis of her right side, she refused to remain silent. Her muffled, stuttered, and frequently incomprehensible orders for the doctors, nurses, and miscellaneous hospital staff were most definitely understood to be just that—orders. Those deficiencies had also cemented Gwyneth's place as the temporary head of all things Van Klein.

Yesterday her mother had been moved to a rehab facility. Her brothers had wanted their mother home with private nurses; Gwyneth wanted her mother in the best place to get the therapy she needed. Finding a facility that was up to Van Klein standards had been anything but easy. That sent Gwyneth's mind wandering in multiple directions. But today, today she had a different mission.

"Grams said you needed my input on something?" Rachel stood in the doorway to her room.

"I do." She reached for the cardboard tube at the side of the vanity she was using as a desk and stood. "Do you have time now?"

Rachel smiled. "I'm all yours."

The two women left the room and headed down the stairs.

"I need a second opinion."

"On?"

"These." She waved the tube at Rachel as they stepped onto the first floor hardwoods. "I need to approve some blueprints and I want an expert opinion."

"You're restoring an old building?"

"No." Leading Rachel into the dining room, she pulled out the large white scrolls and spread them open on the table. "Mother donated to the building fund for the hospital. I decided that I want it used for the new cardiac hospital at the medical center."

"A worthy cause."

"It will include state-of-the-art stroke treatment." She pointed to the first page. "I've authorized a larger donation to get this done sooner than later."

"I'm impressed." Rachel looked down at the papers. "But what can I do?"

For the next few minutes, Gwyneth pointed out the things in the design that bothered her.

"You realize that hospitals are not my skill set?"

"I know. I also know you're good at your job, so a brilliant restoration architect may only be a decent general architect and that beats a lazy medical facility architect any day of the week."

"So you think the architect is lazy?" Rachel leaned forward for a better look.

Gwyneth shrugged. "What I think is that we may be getting rehashed plans, not new ones. There aren't enough of the specifics we asked for."

"We?" Rachel looked over her shoulder at Gwyneth.

"I gave a list of things that I thought could improve to Mother's doctor. In return, he gave me a list of things that he wished the facility had. After spending all week finding a new facility for Mother's rehab, my list grew even longer. The architect promised he'd give us a draft with updates by yesterday."

"These are them?"

She nodded, leaned over and pointed to the parts she thought made no sense. "The architect says this is how it's always done. I'm not buying it."

Mitch knew it was impolite not to announce himself, but he didn't want to interrupt. Or, more accurately, he was thoroughly enjoying watching the woman at the dining room table. To think he'd been afraid that her mother's stroke and the succeeding responsibilities would cripple her. Instead, it had done quite the opposite. She'd become a tiger in the boardroom.

"What you're asking doesn't seem unreasonable." Rachel reached across the table and shifted some pages. "See here? It looks to me like this space could be reconfigured to suit your purposes, but like I said, this isn't my area of expertise."

Gwyneth straightened and bobbed her head. "That's mostly what I was thinking. Thank you for confirming I'm not crazy."

"Any time, and trust me when I say, you're far from crazy." Rachel turned and spotted Mitch. "Oh, I didn't know you were there."

"Just got here." He moved into the room. "Grams is looking for both of you. The guests are expected to arrive shortly and she changed her mind about the table centerpieces and needs some extra hands to rearrange things. And for the record, she refused my help."

Gwyneth bit back a chuckle, but Rachel had no such interest in protecting his pride. "Smart woman." She took one step before pausing at Gwyneth's side. "You're on the right track. Keep pushing until they give you what you want."

Leaving the room, Rachel leaned in to kiss him on the cheek as she walked past, softly whispering, "We may have created a monster."

He knew what she meant. Gwyneth Van Klein was quickly garnering a reputation as a formidable opponent. The politician in him liked that. He was horribly proud of how she was finally taking charge of her own life, but didn't dare say it out loud.

Carefully rolling the scattered pages and placing them in the cardboard tube, she turned to face him. "We'd better hurry to help Lila."

Mitch stood frozen in place, studying her.

Using her free hand to touch her nose, she frowned at him. "Do I have something on my face?"

"Are you really the same woman who just a few weeks ago informed me she couldn't choose her own wardrobe and yet, here you are, designing hospitals?"

Thankfully, she took his words in stride and chuckled. "I wouldn't go so far as to say I'm designing the hospital, but it will be great when it's done."

Through the window he could see the first limousine with Washington passengers had arrived. "And the dog and pony show begins."

"Let's do it." She bumped his shoulder with hers and practically sashayed out of the room. His cousin was right. They'd created a monster. Of sorts.

The day couldn't have been going better if he'd scripted the event. Every one of the fifteen senators and congressmen he'd invited to the social gathering had both accepted the invitation and actually shown up.

The mini rodeo they'd arranged in the corrals by the barn for their out-of-state guests had been a smashing success. As much as everyone seemed to love the barbecue, no one could stop talking about the bronco busting. Of course, the ranch hands who had participated in the events made a point to wear their biggest prize belt buckles, giving his colleagues even more to talk about. A few of the hands who were good at trick roping were meandering through the guests showing off their talents. Laughter and jokes were flowing freer than the liquor.

"Did Senator Jenkins say anything to you?" Standing beside him, Gwyneth took a slow sip of lemonade as she surveyed guests and family.

"No, why?"

"I saw her talking to Orlando."

The waiter who, though a legal resident now, had paid a coyote—a smuggler—to get him over the border. "Do you think he shared everything about his story?"

Her lips tipped up in a smile. "I may have stopped to adjust my sandal while standing within earshot."

"You little sneak," he teased.

"A girl has to do what a girl has to do."

He laughed. "And?"

"All I heard was the part about paying fifteen thousand to cross the border and being escorted by armed cartel to ensure they made it."

"That's enough." He looked in the direction of where Katherine Jenkins stood in a huddle with two other senators.

"And look." She grabbed his arm and pointed with her chin at another of their invited guests. "How much do you want to guess Jose is telling him the same story he told us about how illegal criminals are scaring the heck out of the immigrant community?"

Looking at the conversation one of their ranch hands was having with his colleague, and the contorted expressions on the older man's face, he'd bet Gwyneth's idea was a home run. Turning on his heel, he leaned in, kissed her on the cheek, and grinned. "You're a genius."

Her cheeks blushed and she smiled back at him. "The idea made sense."

"I'm telling you," he waved his hands in the air, "you should go into politics."

"No thank you. I have enough on my plate." Looking over his shoulder, her eyes opened wide and her smile grew. "You'll have to excuse me, I need to talk to Leah about something. I'll be back shortly."

The logical thing to do now would be to mingle with the rest of his guests, answer any questions that might pop up after their conversation with the former illegals they had working the event. Instead, all he wanted to do was watch Gwyneth in action.

"She's quite a force to be reckoned with." Susan came

up beside him. "You've been avoiding me."

He shook his head. "Just been busy."

"Mmhm." Her gaze wandered in the same direction as Gwyneth. "You know," she turned to face him, "all this time I thought I was competing with the memory of a dead woman."

"Susan—"

She raised an open palm hand at him. "No need." Her gaze darted to Gwyneth and back. "I can see now that my competition is very much alive, and I don't stand a chance. You look at her like a woman on a diet eyes a German chocolate cake. I wish you both the best, and I will be backing the legislation."

"You have it all wrong."

Before he could explain further, Susan shook her head at him. "For the first time in a long time I think I'm finally seeing the light. You're in love with a living breathing woman." She sighed and turned away. "I'd better go see what I can do to persuade Katherine to join the dark side. Catch you later."

In love with Gwyneth? *In love?* His gaze searched for her in the distance and his heart gave an unexpected kick when he spotted her talking to his cousin Leah. Staring for a long minute, he stopped to consider the last few weeks, when she turned in his direction, spotted him, and she smiled, his heart went into double time. Dear Lord, Susan was right. He was most definitely, profoundly, in love with Gwyneth Van Klein. The next question for him to ponder is now what?

CHAPTER SIXTEEN

"The tea you requested, Miss Gwyneth." Nora carried a tray with a warm mug of tea. When her mother ran the house, she insisted on having the staff serve tea in all its formal glory. Gwyneth, on the other hand, had no time for pouring her own tea and adding milk and sugar to her liking. Instead, she'd given Nora permission to prepare her warm drink to her liking and serve it in a good old-fashioned large mug rather than the delicate porcelain cups her mother used.

"Thank you, Nora."

"My pleasure, miss." Nora hesitated a moment, then flashed a shaky smile. "If I may say something?"

"Of course." Gwyneth reached for the mug.

"You look good behind that desk. It suits you."

Suits her? Blowing on the hot brew, she let the sound of those words roll around in her head a moment. Oddly, not very long ago she would have argued. "Thank you, Nora."

"You're welcome, miss." Turning, Nora quietly left the room.

One of the oddest things for Gwyneth to get used to the last couple of months had been sitting at her father's desk. Since his death, the office/library had hardly ever been used. Once in a blue moon she'd see her mother at the desk, but she preferred to do correspondence from the smaller desk in her bedroom.

As Gwyneth grew to understand all her responsibilities since her mother's stroke, she found spreading out on the large desk worked best for her, so she'd made her father's office her own. It had taken her a good long time to get a handle on all the dealings, but she was finally comfortable with making decisions, and it seemed to show. For the most part, she no longer second-guessed herself at every turn— yes, she doubted her own judgment from time to time, but having Mitch at her side every step of the way encouraging and reassuring her had made all the difference in the world. If she were honest with herself, she doubted she would have found the strength to do half the things she'd done without his positive outlook and absolute faith in her.

So much had changed in her since the gala. At this point, she was also no longer startled by her own reflection in mirrors as she walked through the house. At first seeing herself in shoulder-length hair with shapely eyebrows and a hint of make up the way Eve had taught her to apply it, had been rather jarring. Now she felt more at home in her own skin than she ever had before.

"Yes, Alfred. I understand, but I feel that selling our shares would be more in line with my mother's vision for the family." Tapping the fingers of her left hand on the desktop, she tried not to roll her eyes as their broker prattled on over her investment changes. Shifting the handset to her left hand, she scribbled on her to-do list *transfer stock accounts*. At first she'd listened carefully to everything Alfred had to say, but it hadn't taken her long to realize his management skills were directly related to the commissions he'd earn and not necessarily what was in her family's best interest. As it turned out, tinkering with the market and tracking current assets and potential stock buys was something she truly enjoyed, and even appeared to be good at. A skill she'd no doubt inherited from her father. As smart as Prudence Van Klein was, it was Gwyneth's feeling that her mother had allowed herself to be guided solely on Alfred's advice rather than following the market herself.

The doorbell rang and immediately, her heart began beating in double time. Mitch was set to pick her up at five o'clock. As usual, he was precisely on time. "Alfred, my next appointment has arrived. Please take care of the order I've put in and I will follow up in the morning." She'd kept a polite smile on her face during the entire conversation in hopes it would relay a more pleasant tone. Now all she wanted was to get off the phone and see Mitch.

Senator Mitchell Baron was the last one of the changes she'd become used to. To her delight, after the big gala, after her mother was moved to rehab, after she'd gotten a handle on the guilt she'd initially felt and begun to deal with the challenges of her new role in the family business, Mitch had not disappeared. As a matter of fact, he'd become a staple in her life. The first month he'd call every day and see her every weekend. By the second month, it had become the norm for her to join the Barons for their weekly Sunday family dinner, and spend every day that Mitch was in town with him. She'd seen more of Houston and its surroundings in the last month than she had in her entire life.

Oliver appeared in the foyer as Gwyneth returned the handset to its place, disconnecting the call. Pushing to her feet, she called out, "No need, Oliver. I'll get the door."

Stopping in his tracks, the butler bobbed his head. "Yes, Miss Gwyneth."

Gwyneth had to stop herself from running to the door, but she couldn't stop from flinging it open.

"Hey, beautiful." That was one word she'd finally gotten used to and was pretty sure she'd never grow tired of.

"Hey." She knew she was smiling from ear to ear and wondered why her face hadn't cracked after two months of smiling at Mitch. But the best part was that she'd gone from a pity escort to a real date to dating.

His arms slipped around her waist, and tugging her closer, his head dipped and his lips captured hers in a perfect toe curling kiss. Easing back, he kept his arms around her middle. "How's my girl today?"

"About to fire Mother's stockbroker."

"Atta girl." He smiled.

"You don't like my stockbroker either?"

"Don't know him. But if you think he needs to go, then I'm on your side."

And there he was, the best thing to ever happen to her. She didn't dare think what would happen when his interest waned and he moved on, but she wasn't going to go there now. She was going to live in the moment and enjoy it as if it were the last. Then she was going to pray that nothing ever changed.

"Are you ready?" Standing in the foyer of Gwyneth's home, Mitch hoped his smile didn't look as shaky as he felt. He'd spent all morning staring at the clock, counting the minutes ticking by until it was time to pick her up.

"Yes, sir." She turned and grabbed her handbag from a nearby bench.

"Is that new?" For the life of him he couldn't remember what was there before, but he'd have sworn it was not a vintage upholstered bench.

She nodded. "Picked it up last week when I was running some errands. There was a sidewalk sale near my meeting and this was outside an antique store. I thought it was perfect for the foyer. So much brighter than the dark mahogany church pew that had been here."

Little by little she'd done a few things to brighten the place up. Starting with something as simple as opening the drapes every morning. His hand on the small of her back, he escorted her out the door. "Looks nice."

"I'm so hungry I could eat a horse." Buckling her safety belt, she settled into the front seat of the car. "I just love dinners with your family. My brothers were all married and out of the house by the time I was old enough to eat dinner in the dining room. It's so much fun having so many people to talk to and share your day with."

"Some days it can be a bit much, but I love every one of that crazy big family." He could not imagine growing up as an only child. His family meant everything to him. And now, so did Gwyneth.

"Anything new with your mother?"

"Not really. She's making fewer pouty faces and nodding more, and she's mumbling *yes* much more often without first sputtering *no.*"

"Sounds like she's adjusting to more than her condition."

"I believe she is. She's trying to say more words, and I seem to be the only one who can understand her, but I'm not kidding myself." She chuckled. "Mother is still firmly planted in the last century."

"Early last century," he added, delighted to hear Gwyneth laugh.

"Yes. Early last century. The thing that I still can't understand is how did she know I would be able to handle all the responsibility she's given me."

"Have you asked her?"

She nodded. "Sort of. I asked why me and not one of my brothers."

"What did she say?"

"That I was smarter. But, how could she possibly know that when I was never allowed to do anything on my own."

"I don't have kids, but I've been around some who, even when only a couple of years old, it was clear that they would be a force to reckon with some day. Maybe your mother saw something in you at an early age that she never saw in your brothers?"

"I suppose."

It still boggled his mind what a difference a couple of months could make. With every day, Gwyneth's self-confidence had grown in leaps and bounds. He honestly felt no matter what Prudence said or did from now on, Gwyneth would be perfectly capable of standing her ground. Even her own brothers had come around to treating Gwyneth as more of an equal than a child to be brushed aside.

For the remainder of the drive, she filled him in on the challenges she was having with some people accepting the new business woman in her, while others were cheerfully embracing her participation and the changes she was bringing to the Van Klein philanthropic efforts. Especially the new cardiology wing at the hospital for long-term rehab. The amount of money that Gwyneth had authorized to move the project ahead was astounding even to him. He couldn't be more proud of her.

Pulling into the circle drive in front of the ranch, he put the car in park and hopped out. "I need to run to the barn a minute. We have a mare in labor and I want to check on her before we sit down for dinner. Do you want to wait inside or come with me?"

"I'll come with you."

He extended his hand to her, delighted with the feel of her delicate hand in his. He'd barely crossed into the barn when Mack, the ranch foreman, appeared with a wiry smile on his face.

"Got a surprise for you."

He came to a stop in front of Mack, but didn't let go of Gwyneth's hand. Looking quickly over Mack's shoulder, Mitch smiled at how much things had changed. He still loved coming to the barn and working with the animals, but it was no longer an escape for him, now it was just one more thing to be thankful for. Funny how having Gwyneth in his life had made everything a whole lot brighter. "I'm hoping that grin means it's a good one?"

The foreman nodded, then tipped his head to one side, pointing to the back. "Go look for yourself."

Together, they strolled down several feet, until they reached the larger stalls for laboring animals. To his surprise, one little head peeked out from around the mare's legs. "Wow. That was fast."

His hand was on the gate to unlatch it and go inside when Mack chuckled. "Better take a closer look."

"Oh, my." Gwyneth's free hand rose to her mouth.

Mitch followed her gaze. "*Oh* is right."

From around Mama's front legs, another little head appeared.

"Twins," Gwyneth called out gleefully.

As he slowly approached, the mare flared her nostrils at him, and then lowered her head. Luna was one of his favorite horses and the way she nudged her head against him made him think perhaps he was one of her favorite humans. "You did good, Mama. Your babies are beautiful."

The horse lifted her head and dropped it back, making a gentle snorting sound.

"She does look proud of herself." Gwyneth leaned up against him. "Do you think she'd mind if I rubbed her jaw?"

He shook his head. "I think she'd love it."

What he regretted was that Gwyneth let go of his hand when she took a step forward. Approaching slowly, she lifted one hand to run the side of Luna's jaw. "You have very pretty babies, Mama. That was hard work. You did a good job."

The horse blinked at her, slightly pushing her head against Gwyneth's hand.

"That means thank you."

"Oh, sweet girl," Gwyneth cooed. "We're very proud of you."

This time Luna moved her head and brushed up against Gwyneth, making her laugh.

"You're welcome. I know every girl likes to know she's appreciated."

Mitch sidled up beside Gwyneth. "You are."

She glance at him over her shoulder. "Yes, she is."

"Not Luna." He inched closer, putting his finger under Gwyneth's chin and lifting it in his direction. "You, Miss Gwyneth Van Klein, are very much appreciated."

"Oh." She blinked. "That's, uhm, sweet of you to say."

He took one more step, closing the small distance between them. "It's not sweet. It's the truth. You are appreciated," he swallowed hard, here went nothing. "And loved."

Her mouth fell slightly open and she blinked, twice.

"In case you missed it, I love you."

Now her mouth snapped shut and her eyes popped open wide. "You love me?"

Letting his finger softly run down the side of her jaw, he nodded. "Full disclosure. I'm very much in love with you."

Water glistened in her eyes as she blinked back the threat of tears.

Not the reaction he was expecting. Panic laced with fear licked at his insides. "I'm sorry if that's—"

Shaking her head frantically, her finger landed on his lips. "I've never heard anything so beautiful in my life. These are happy tears."

"They are?" Did his voice just squeak?

She nodded. "And full disclosure. I'm very much in love with you too."

"If you don't kiss her now, I will." Mack stood a few yards away grinning.

"My mother didn't raise a fool." Pulling her into the tight fold of his arms, he lowered his lips to meet hers.

Somewhere in the back of his mind he heard boot heels clicking against the concrete floor as Mack left the barn muttering something about "Another one bites the dust."

EPILOGUE

"I adore the beach." Rachel took in a long, deep breath. "Don't you just love the smell of the ocean?"

Nodding her head, Lila Baron smiled at her granddaughter. "We really should come to Galveston more often. Especially now that Chase has added on to the resort."

"I can't believe I haven't been here since cousin Andrew's wedding. We should celebrate the Governor's birthday here every year."

"I was thinking the same thing." Mitch came up behind the two women and kissed each on the cheek, adding a quick hug for his grandmother. "Have either of you two seen Gwyneth?"

Rachel shook her head. "If y'all are going to have any future together, you really need to stop losing her."

"Ha, ha, ha." Mitch scanned the large oceanside restaurant. "Found her."

Both Rachel and her grandmother kept their gazes on Mitch as he practically trotted across the large veranda to where Gwyneth was chatting with Eve and Paige.

"I never thought I'd see the day." Their grandmother smiled into the distance. "I honestly thought that light in his eyes was forever dimmed when we lost Abbie."

"I know what you mean." Whenever Rachel spotted her cousin staring off into the distance, which the last few years was rather often, she knew he was either thinking of what was or what might have been. For the better part of the last year, that faraway look had been replaced by a constant twinkle that flared into a full on sparkle whenever he set his eyes on Gwyneth.

If anyone had told Rachel one year ago that ugly duckling Gwyneth Van Klein would turn into a fashionable swan and win Mitch's heart, she'd have asked the person what were they smoking. And yet, here they were. From where Rachel sat, she could see the two making the rounds, hand in hand, smiling and chatting with the family and guests.

"You two look awfully content." Leah came to sit with her sister and grandmother. "Where's the Governor?"

"He'll be back any moment. Had something to talk to your brother about."

"Which brother?" Leah asked.

"Devlin." Grams sighed. "I suspect he is not so subtly singing Emily's praises."

"I suppose that's better than the *you-know-what or get off the pot* speech we usually get." Rachel knew better than to use the S word around her grandmother, even if the Governor used it with some regularity.

"I don't know." Leah shrugged. "After all these years, I don't think there's anything more there than a good friendship. You know, like Jack and Eve. He was her plus-one for years. Now Jack is madly in love with Siobhan and Eve is happily married to Jared. If you ask me, the Governor is wasting his breath."

Her sister had a point, but finding a forever kind of love was much easier said than done. It wasn't like she didn't want to have a man look at her the way her cousin Mitch was looking at Gwyneth. Even now, seeing them walking toward the table, smiling, bumping shoulders and laughing gave Rachel goosebumps.

"They do make a cute couple, don't they?" Leah was watching the two approach as well. "It's good to see him happy again."

"Amen." Grams bobbed her head moments before Mitch and Gwyneth joined them.

"Where's the Governor?" Mitch held the chair for Gwyneth before taking a seat beside her.

"Talking to Devlin," Rachel volunteered.

Lips tightly pressed, Mitch bit back a laugh.

"What's so funny?" Gwyneth asked.

"Nothing." Doing his best to put on a straight face, Mitch shrugged. "When our grandfather is in Marine mode on a mission, it can be hard standing your ground."

"I repeat." Gwyneth dipped her head to one side. "What's so funny?"

Mitch reached for her hand, folded it in his, and ran his thumb gently along the side of her palm. "Have I mentioned lately that I love you?"

"I love you back, but quit dodging the question."

Gwyneth's quick response had Rachel and her sister chuckling under their breath. Mitch had clearly met his match, and clearly was loving every minute at Gwyneth's side.

"It's nothing, only Devlin was just saying how relieved he was that with so many of us having gotten engaged or married this year that the Governor would finally get off his back about his friendship with Emily."

That made Gwyneth chuckle a little harder before biting her lips to stifle the laughter. "Sorry, but I always thought Devlin was pretty smart."

"He thinks so," Leah added quickly.

"He is," Grams spoke up. "Just not when it comes to anticipating his grandfather's determination."

"Oh. My. Lord." Leah's eyes bugged out of her head.

"What?" Rachel tried to follow the direction of her sister's gaze, her own finally landing on Gwyneth. A single round solitaire diamond sparkled from her left hand. Without hesitation, she sprang from her seat and ran around to hug first Mitch then, Gwyneth. "Talk about close-mouthed."

"We thought it would be a nice birthday gift for the Governor." Mitch squeezed his fiancée's hand.

"Too bad y'all didn't tell him before he cornered Devlin." Leah came around the table and hugged the happy couple. "Congratulations. I couldn't be happier."

More than any of their siblings or cousins finding their soulmates, Mitch having a second chance at true love was enough to make their little corner of the world a much happier place.

"There's something else you're not telling us." Their grandmother stared intently at Mitch.

Taking a moment to face his fiancée, Mitch seemed to communicate without words as Gwyneth shrugged. How Rachel wished she could find someone who knew what she was thinking simply by the look in her eyes.

"I've decided not to run for re-election." Mitch almost seemed to be holding his breath as his words settled around the table.

Grams frowned. "You're sure?"

Once again, he looked at Gwyneth and smiling back at him, she gave an almost undetectable nod.

"I don't want to be commuting to DC anymore."

His grandmother sighed. "Fair enough."

"I'm going to run for the Texas Senate." He shifted in his seat, inching a little closer to Gwyneth and draped his arm around her shoulder. "I want to be closer to home."

A contented twinkle appeared in Grams' eyes.

"We're not getting any younger," Mitch started.

Playfully, Gwyneth slapped him on the arm. "Speak for yourself."

Chuckling loudly, he stared at her just long enough to convey how much he loved her. "We were thinking of a small wedding, just the family—"

"I thought you said small," Leah teased.

Mitch ignored his cousin. "Next month."

"Next month?" Rachel hadn't meant to express her surprise out loud. "That's a little fast, don't you think?"

The two shook their heads.

"I don't need a big fancy wedding." The way Gwyneth stared up at Mitch made Rachel wonder if she would ever find a man to fall that deeply in love with.

"What does Prudence have to say about all this?" Though her expression was calm and serene, everyone at the table understood why Grams had to even ask. Prudence Van Klein was not an easy woman and the stroke had done little to soften her stuffy nature.

"She's actually quite pleased." Gwyneth smiled. "Though I suspect more so about being related to you than about my getting married."

"Nonsense." Grams smiled. "Does she know about the short engagement?"

"We thought we'd give her time to get used to the idea of our engagement first."

Grams bobbed her head. "Probably a good idea."

"Someone needs to give that man grandchildren." Devlin gave his grandmother a quick peck on the cheek and collapsed into the nearby empty chair. "I can't take too many more of the Governor's lectures on the joys of marriage and fatherhood."

At her brother's words, Mitch and Gwyneth leveled their gazes on each other and the corners of their mouths tipped up in the sweetest of smiles. If Rachel were a betting woman, her money would be on a wedding in one month and a baby in nine more. Yep. Mitch was about to get his chance at the whole enchilada: wife, kids, and happily ever after. And wasn't that the best news ever.

Enjoy an excerpt from
Just One Mistake

Some days the opulence of the Memorial Country Club reminded Rachel Baron that despite her ordinary job, her world was one of privilege and high expectations. The gathering of the county's most elite members of society filled the air with the sound of laughter, clinking glasses and as always, the buzz of intimate conversation.

Under the warm glow of the massive crystal chandeliers, she moved gracefully through the crowds in a determined effort to cross the ballroom. Pausing every few feet to exchange pleasantries and air-kisses with the Houston socialites who had known her since childhood, she willed her empty stomach not to grumble. Tables of what she knew would be delicious hors d'oeuvres, were getting closer and closer. If only she didn't have to make nice with so many people. The professional upside of being the granddaughter of a former governor, and cousin of a current well loved senator, included cutting through red tape and accessing hard to find supplies for any of her restoration projects. The downside meant that no matter how hungry she was, stopping to be nice to everyone who recognized her was her only option.

"Rachel, dear. That dress is simply stunning." An older brunette, whose gray roots were well camouflaged and had been a staple at her grandparents' fundraisers for the many charities her family supported, smiled widely and stepped in for another of those air kisses that Rachel detested. "I love the way the color brings out the green in your eyes."

"How sweet of you to say. You look quite smashing yourself."

The woman puffed up like a peacock. "I had luncheon this week at Emily Whitestone's. You did a marvelous job on her remodel. The way you blended the old and new was seamless. Absolutely wonderful."

Now that made her smile in earnest. The project had been a combination restoration of an outdated kitchen and dining as well as including an addition that needed to blend in with the integrity of the 1930's home, as well as embrace a modern lifestyle. "Thank you. It was a fun project." She really had enjoyed this particular project, enough to continue politely chatting about it despite the table of food calling her name.

By the time her grandmother's friend had moved on to someone else, Rachel finally reached the table she'd been eyeing all evening, her gaze dancing between the bacon wrapped shrimp, the caviar fountain, and a few things that she had no clue what they were, but she was hungry enough to sample all of it.

"Skip dinner again?" Her cousin Mitch, the senator, who she simply adored, came up beside her.

"What makes you say that?"

He smiled. "You're looking at everything the way a kid would eye a banana split."

"Have you tried any of it?"

"The shrimp is quite good and Gwyneth loves the quinoa balls."

Her gaze shifted to the plate filled with crusty round balls. "Oh, that's what those are."

"One of these days someone's going to serve pigs in a blanket and find a mad rush from us guys who like meat and potatoes."

An eruption of laughter escaped her throat before she could slap a hand over her mouth. Looking over her shoulder, she leaned in and lowered her voice. "I wouldn't mind a few now myself."

"Have you heard about the Hartwig House?"

One of her passions was the architectural history of old Houston. The Hartwig House had been an opulent family home, a showpiece along what had once been referred to as

Millionaire's Row. That is until the last Hartwig died off without heirs and the once beautiful old home fell into neglect and disrepair. "What about it? Did someone finally buy it?"

"Not exactly." Mitch looked around. "The city condemned it."

"Oh, no." Her shoulders slumped with disappointment. Rachel hated the way society so easily tore down older structures to bring in the new. If it were up to the local authorities, all the masterful constructions of Europe would be replaced with new century modern blocks. "That should be a crime."

"That's what I said." Gwyneth sidled up beside her fiancé and ignoring the social norms of public displays of affection, gave him a quick peck on the lips before turning to face Rachel. "Lilian Prentiss told me about the, and I quote, *ugly boarded up eyesore and magnet for every vagrant west of the Mississippi* finally being removed from her neighborhood. So I checked with Councilman Bates. She got it half right."

"What half?" Rachel resisted the urge to cross her fingers and say a prayer for the poor old house.

"The city finally has ownership of the property and the health department and city engineers all agree it's not safe and has to come down. It is indeed on the list to be condemned and razed."

"Short sighted—" Before she could finish her unladylike thought, her future cousin-in-law cut her off.

"This is the half I think you'll like. The city has a new program for restoring abandoned buildings before they're torn down."

Rachel frowned running through all the government programs she'd dealt with, wondering which might come into play.

"Anyone willing to restore the homes within one year can purchase the distressed properties for one dollar."

"Wait," Rachel shook her head, "isn't that for low income neighborhoods? The ones that are prone to meth houses and gang hangouts?"

Still smiling, Gwyneth nodded. "It is, but, there's nothing in the program that specifies the size or location of the distressed home, so Mayor Borden is going to add it to the list of homes going on the auction block."

The allure of rescuing such a historic gem resonated with everything in her. All she'd seen in recent years was the jungle like appearance of the old building hidden far behind the walled front gates. If the inside was as bad as the outside, the undertaking would be gargantuan.

"I recognize that glint." Mitch rolled his eyes skyward. "Heaven help us, but I told Gwyneth you'd find such a project irresistible."

Irresistible. He was certainly right about that, but deep down, she wanted more than to simply do the designs, or oversee the restoration. Rachel wanted full control of the project. To ensure that her designs were not vetoed by the owner and that she had the right to hire or fire anyone involved who didn't live up to her expectations.

"Told you she couldn't resist." Mitch wound his arm around Gwyneth's waist. "Am I right?"

Was he right? Could she pass it up? Could she do this on her own? Or was she completely nuts for even considering it? A hard smile tugged at the corner of her lips. "You'd better believe it." Bringing that old girl back to her days of splendor and glory was going to be the most fun she'd ever had!

MEET CHRIS

USA TODAY Bestselling Author of dozens of contemporary novels, including the award winning Aloha Series, Chris Keniston lives in suburban Dallas with her husband, two human children, and two canine children. Though she loves her puppies equally, she admits being especially attached to her German Shepherd rescue. After all, even dogs deserve a happily ever after.

More on Chris and all her books can be found at
www.chriskeniston.com

Follow Chris' Monday Blog at her website
ChrisKenistonAuthor

Follow Chris on Facebook at
ChrisKenistonAuthor

Never miss a New Release!
Sign up for News from Chris:
www.chriskeniston.com/newsletter.html

Questions? Comments?
I would love to hear from you! You can reach me at:
chris@chriskeniston.com

www.ingramcontent.com/pod-product-compliance
Lightning Source LLC
Chambersburg PA
CBHW031543310726
48971CB00008B/2608